SHIMMER

SHIMMER

THE FAIRHAVEN CHRONICLES BOOK TWO

MARTHA CARR

MICHAEL ANDERLE

DISRUPTIVE IMAGINATION

Copyright © 2017 Martha Carr and Michael Anderle
Cover Art by Jake @ J Caleb Design
http://jcalebdesign.com / jcalebdesign@gmail.com
Cover copyright © LMBPN Publishing

LMBPN Publishing
PMB 196, 2540 South Maryland Pkwy
Las Vegas, NV 89109

First US edition, November 2017
Version 1.11 January 2020
Print ISBN: 978-1-64202-799-0

SHIMMER TEAM

Thanks to the JIT Readers

Alex Wilson
Kelly ODonnell
Jed Moulton
Micky Cocker
AbH Belxjander Draconis Serechai
Larry Omans
Kimberly Boyer
Paul Westman
Joshua Ahles

If I've missed anyone, please let me know!

Editor
Lynne Stiegler

DEDICATIONS

From Martha

*To everyone who still believes in magic and all the possibilities
that holds. To all the readers who make this ride so much fun.
And to all the readers just like me who create wonder, big and
small, every day.*

From Michael

*To Family, Friends and
Those Who Love
To Read.
May We All Enjoy Grace
To Live The Life We Are
Called.*

CHAPTER ONE

Deep within the tunnels beneath the magical city of Fairhaven, Victoria dodged a brilliant blast of green light as it ricocheted off the glowing crystals embedded in the walls. The blast had nearly hit her square in the face. Smoke sizzled from a burn mark on the rock inches from her face, evidence of what would have happened to her if she had been even a little bit slower.

Time to get to cover.

Half her little training cavern was filled with shimmering purple grass, and not far away a waterfall crashed into a small lake. The grass stung anything it touched, but it was the better option. She ducked another blast of light and rolled into the grass with seconds to spare. The soft tips of the grass stung her like hundreds of bees, but she gritted her teeth and kept low. Her skin itched, and she could already feel the welts swelling on her arms and face.

I can't worry about the pain. Her primary focus was to stay out of sight, especially since a green blast would hurt a hell of a lot more than some stinging grass. Besides, the black magic in her blood would heal her welts as soon as she wasn't under fire anymore.

"You found cover! Good thinking, Victoria!" Fyrn shouted across the cavern.

Man, sometimes I hate training. She always walked away with bruises, but it would all be worth it in the end.

Every day she got better, and every day her wizard mentor's attacks got stronger. He was trying to make her a better fighter, trying to give her everything she needed to succeed and stay alive in a city that didn't quite trust her.

Fyrn won't throw anything at me I can't handle, but damn! *Sometimes I wish he didn't trust me so much.*

Another blast hummed through the air, singeing a few loose locks of her hair as it passed. The energy fizzled against the cave wall, leaving another black mark in its wake.

In today's training exercise Victoria had only one mission. *Don't get caught.* She could be seen, she could banter, but she couldn't get hit. This lesson was about speed and agility, not to mention how to escape a bad situation if she couldn't win a fight. Not that it would ever happen, of course. She gained more control over the magical artifact in her arm with every day that passed.

Fyrn tried to hide his reactions, but she saw his impressed grins. He had to be pleased with how quickly she was picking up and mastering her new gifts.

"Let's up the stakes!" Fyrn shouted.

She groaned. Pain almost always followed that sentence.

A sequence of attacks sailed toward her, one after the other, each aimed for a different part of her body. She called these 'combos,' and she fucking hated them. One of them hit her every single time.

Every. Single. Time.

She dodged the first two, twisting out of the way with only a second to spare as they hit the wall and fizzled. The third came dangerously close to her head, and she could feel the heat from the fourth as it sailed past her nose.

The fifth, of course, hit her square in the chest.

Struck by the full force of a wizard's power beam, Victoria flew backward and hit the wall hard. Pain splintered up her back and something in her shoulders cracked. She whimpered, sliding to the ground as her world went fuzzy. She tried to stand, but ended up on her hands and knees when her feet gave out underneath her.

The cold tip of a crystal pressed into her forehead, indenting her skin as Fyrn claimed victory. When her vision cleared, Victoria saw nothing but the wizard's long staff and the glimmering crystal at its tip. If he were a real adversary, he could have blown her head off and ended the fight.

"Yeah, yeah, you win. Big—" She stopped as his face came into focus. Brows furrowed, eyes narrowed in hatred, pupils dilated—he looked ready to kill.

And the full weight of his glare was focused squarely on her.

"Fyrn?" she said warily, trying to snap him out of it.

Blinking rapidly, the old wizard lowered his staff and stepped away. His shoulders drooped, and he stared at her for a few moments. Victoria cautiously stood, confused and a little worried that her mentor could look at her with such hatred.

"I got caught up in the moment." He turned his back on her, leaning on the staff as he walked toward the waterfall. The meadow of purple grass between them made him seem small, but Victoria knew better. This wizard was easily the most powerful in Fairhaven. His knowledge, experience, and abilities dwarfed any of the other wizards who lived in Fairhaven.

Truth be told, Fyrn could kill her. She would put up one hell of a fight and maybe take him with her, but it was unlikely she would win in a fight against her mentor. And until now, she hadn't thought she would ever need to worry about that.

But the look in his eyes had been deadly. Even if he had merely been caught up in the moment, he had looked ready to kill.

And to many people in the magical world, Victoria was someone worth killing.

Victoria studied the magical steampunk-style dagger that had fused with her right forearm the day Luak had murdered her parents. This was dark magic, and Fyrn had confessed that these artifacts often corrupted the people who bonded with them. Hopefully that wouldn't happen to her.

Hopefully, Fyrn would never *need* to kill her.

On a little boulder by the exit, Styx clapped and cheered in the gibberish language of the pixies. Wings flapping, he soared into the air and flitted around her head, chittering the whole way. She chuckled at the little creature's antics. "No more coffee for you, kiddo. *Jesus.*"

Fyrn tapped his staff against the mossy ground in his

version of applause. "Take the rest of the day off. Rest. Recharge. You did well today, Victoria."

"I should keep training." She looked forward to the day when she didn't need to train constantly, but she knew it wouldn't come for a while. Come hell or high water, she would have revenge on Luak for murdering her parents. *He* wouldn't rest, and neither should she.

Fyrn shook his head, his long white beard trailing a bit behind with every motion. "Every good warrior must know when to rest as well as when to fight. Exhausting yourself isn't going to make you better than Luak, so go home."

"I need to get stronger, Fyrn."

"Exactly, and exhausting yourself isn't going to do that. Do you even listen when I speak? Good lord, child. You need to get physically stronger, to the point where you can hold both the sword and shield at the same time. Right now you can barely hold one."

"So make me do pushups! Make me lift weights, or run laps. Going home and resting isn't going to make me stronger."

"No, but it will let me look for a spell or something. Physically, you simply aren't strong enough. You will *never* be strong enough for that artifact, Victoria. No human *could* be. There are limitations to the human body that you can't overcome, regardless of how hard you train. I saw your father go through these struggles, and watching you go through the same ordeal is only driving home the point."

"Lame."

"Quite."

"Well, what options do we have? Only spells? Hey, is there another Rhazdon Artifact that can make me stronger?" She chuckled, but her smile quickly faded. If she were being honest with herself, it wasn't a joke at all. Another artifact would certainly speed up her training.

"Absolutely not!" Fyrn's voice echoed in the cave like thunder over a desert, hard and loud. Panicked, Styx dove into Victoria's hair, his tiny body trembling as he clung to her.

"Fyrn, I was kidding. I don't want—"

"Dark magic is not something to joke about, Victoria. It kills. It corrupts. You may not lose control of yourself like some Rhazdon hosts do, but every host I've ever seen loses themselves to bloodlust and a thirst for power. Look at Luak! How many people do you think he's killed?"

She balled her hands in anger, but she didn't know what to say.

Fyrn continued, scowling. "If you don't take dark magic seriously, it will destroy you from within. I don't know if anyone has ever had more than one Rhazdon Artifact except for Rhazdon himself, and he started a war that killed thousands! I won't let you become him!"

Victoria lifted her hands in gentle surrender. "I'm sorry, Fyrn. I take it back."

"I'll find you a spell. We have other options." Fyrn stroked his beard, but something in the old wizard's face had shifted. As she watched him gaze around the cave, Victoria wondered how much he believed what he was saying. Maybe deep in his heart he suspected what she was already beginning to believe: no spell was going to help her.

She had to face the facts. Spells had limits the Rhazdon Artifacts didn't have.

Even when she had mastered the Rhazdon Artifact in her arm, she wouldn't be strong enough to actively wield the weapons she summoned. It wouldn't do any good for her to have the knowledge but no practical ability to use it. She needed some kind of supplement, some way to get stronger than any human ever could, and so far it seemed like only another Rhazdon Artifact could do that.

Yes, perhaps getting another would destroy her, but she had a powerful enemy who wanted her dead. He had massacred her parents and set a ravenous snarx loose on the city of Fairhaven, killing dozens. That thing may have had a funny name, but it had been nothing to laugh at when it had decapitated Fairhaven citizens and left orphans in its wake. If Victoria hadn't put her life on the line, the king would have let his people die. Or worse, Luak might have taken over and killed hundreds more.

This was life or death.

Anyway, it wasn't as if she could go out and shop for a second Rhazdon Artifact. She would wait to see what Fyrn came up with, but the dark magic in her body had so far done only good. She had saved Fairhaven from the snarx, and been welcomed by many of its citizens—though not all —as a hero. Maybe the magic of the Rhazdon Artifacts didn't have the same effect on her as it did for others, or maybe it was unjustly feared.

Her powers were all she could use to get her revenge on Luak, and she wouldn't rule out using more dark magic if it meant she got justice for everyone that evil bastard had murdered.

Screw training. Screw patience. Screw inner peace. Victoria needed a break.

During the championship Berserk match for the season, she raced along the city's main Berserk field while the crowd roared on either side of her. They faced the Chezlewok team today. Apparently it was some kind of slithering monster with fangs and a lightning-quick bite.

Didn't matter. They would lose to the Plits.

"Victoria, here!" Audrey waved her hands, pointing to a pair of black fidgets—fifty points each!—rolling near her. She charged for one, and Victoria lunged toward the other.

It slipped out of her fingers as she hit the ground. Audrey fell as well, missing her fidget by a few inches as it scuttled through the grass.

Across the field an ogre snorted, his eyes focused on Audrey's sprawled body.

Oh, shit.

Such was the game, after all: hurt your opponent until they went to the medic and were disqualified from continuing. And boy, did this team love trying to take out the fidget chasers.

He ran toward them, the ground rumbling under his massive feet. It wasn't long before his eight-foot-tall body towered over them—he looked ready to flatten Audrey. She scrambled to stand, but her shoes slipped on the wet ground cover.

Victoria dove for her friend, grabbing her shoulder and rolling them both out of the way seconds before the ogre toppled onto them both.

Audrey grinned. "You're the best."

"I know." Victoria winked.

A green fidget squeaked beneath the ogre's leg, its indestructible body pinned momentarily by the monster. Victoria snatched it free and its tiny feet wriggled like a fish out of water. "A hundred points! Damn!"

An elf on their team—Georgie—sped by and plucked the fidget from Victoria's hands. "Thanks, ladies!"

As the opposing team's ogre pushed himself to his feet, Bertha's brother Edgar plowed into him from the side. Bones cracked, dirt kicked into the air, and Victoria winced in sympathy.

That had to hurt.

Audrey, however, chuckled. "That's what you get for messing with Team Plit!"

"Damn right! Now let's win this thing," Victoria said, fist-bumping her buddy. Her eyes scanned the field for the next fidget.

As they ran through the field of ogres and elves tackling each other, Victoria felt strangely at home. These were her people—her team, her buddies. They would always have her back.

Always.

———

Victoria sat on the floor of the cave she and Audrey had slept in when they first came to Fairhaven. Back propped against the jagged wall, she gently tapped her head against the rock as she tried to make sense of her runaway thoughts. Styx flew in circles above her to wear himself out. Otherwise he would be up all night rummaging through the kitchen cupboards. Victoria might have been rich thanks to her parents' forethought, but this pixie would eat her out of house and home if she wasn't careful.

Even though she had initially brought up finding a second Rhazdon Artifact as a joke, the idea made more sense to her the longer she thought about it.

And that scared her.

She didn't know what worried her more: The idea of having more dark magic pulsing through her veins or the fear that she might be chasing power the same way as others who had been corrupted by the Rhazdon Artifacts fused with their bodies had.

After all, Fyrn had once mentioned how he watched host after host be destroyed by their own greed and lust for power. She could hear the reasoning now: just a little more, and I'll stop. Just a little more, and I'll have enough. Just a little more, and I'll be happy.

Just a little more.

"I wouldn't mind some company," Shiloh said.

Victoria jumped, heart skipping a beat when the ghost tied to her Rhazdon Artifact appeared. He lounged against a boulder, examining his nails in the same bored fashion as always.

"Some company?" she asked.

He nodded. "Get another Rhazdon Artifact ghost for me."

"Wouldn't you just find it boring?"

"Probably, but it's worth a try. Do it, and I might hate you less."

She frowned. "That's a terrible reason to fuse with another Artifact."

"Suit yourself." Shiloh shrugged, and as fast as he had appeared, he disappeared again.

Sometimes she hated that ghost. True, he didn't have a choice about being forever tied to the dagger in her arm, but he didn't have to make her miserable. Lately he had taken to hiding wherever it was ghosts hung out, and she had rather enjoyed the peace. Sometimes she even forgot he existed.

Happy times.

Elbow resting on her knee, Victoria stared at beautiful Fairhaven below her as her mind wandered. The city had become her refuge, the safe space she called home. Luak had threatened them in an effort to take control of the city and she had stopped him, thanks to the power of her Rhazdon Artifact. It, and it alone, had given her the ability to kill the snarx. She couldn't have done that without magic, and she couldn't deny that the dark magic had become a part of her. Being a Rhazdon host was a life sentence, since removing the artifact would kill her. She would never again be without it, so there was no point in hating what she was.

But to add another? That would be pushing her luck.

She sighed, rubbing her eyes as she forced herself to face the bitter truth. Dark magic was dangerous, and she was treading a thin line between greed and having enough power to get justice and do what was right.

If she listened to her heart, she would always make the right choice. And right now it told her to wait.

Victoria would do whatever it took to take care of her

city, her friends, and the magical world that had quickly captured her imagination. She adored Fairhaven, and if it meant destroying herself to save it, that's what she would do.

Until then, she would wait.

CHAPTER TWO

As the overhead crystals in the Fairhaven cavern began to dim, signaling the end of another day, Audrey leaned her elbows on the windowsill and watched the street for Victoria.

The townspeople of Fairhaven had reacted quite surprisingly to Victoria being a Rhazdon host. Half of them seemed to adore her, even thanking her in the street, while the other half kept their distance and watched her suspiciously.

But they had all ignored Audrey.

It wasn't fair. Audrey had fought the snarx too. She had helped drag its head back to town. She had stood on the balcony when Luak threatened Victoria, sword at the ready in case shit went down.

At every step of the way, Audrey had put her life on the line to keep Victoria alive, but no one here cared. As usual, they fawned over Victoria while Audrey stood in her friend's shadow.

She blew a raspberry, forehead pressed against the windowpane.

Around a bend in the street, a mop of braided strawberry blonde hair appeared in the crowd. Victoria. She had several elves in tow, their gorgeous and ornate gowns trailing on the cobblestone street. They fawned over her, laughing at something she said as she wildly gestured with her hands. They had likely asked about her training or her magical exploits, eager to hear stories from a Rhazdon host who was for some reason not actively trying to kill them.

A heroic Rhazdon host was like a horse walking into a supermarket: no one knew quite what to make of it, but everyone wanted a closer look.

Fuck! What Audrey wouldn't give to walk a day in Victoria's shoes. To be adored, respected. Hell, she would settle for being *noticed*.

A pang of guilt shot through Audrey like lightning, and she left her post at the window to pace the room with her hands in her pockets. Part of her wished she could stuff these emotions down deep and pretend they didn't exist... but they did. Resentment and envy burned deep within her soul, and they grew stronger every day as she tried to ignore them.

Curious about what was keeping Victoria, Audrey peeked through the window again to find her friend surrounded by even more people in the middle of the street. Elves and ogres alike mobbed her, hanging on her every word.

Before she could help herself, Audrey scoffed in disgust. The moment the sound escaped her lips, she blushed and clamped a hand over her mouth.

She had to get her jealousy under control.

For now, a walk sounded like a great way to cool off. She trotted down the stairs and out the back door to avoid Victoria and her fans, not quite in the mood to deal with crowds or be reminded of her envy.

The thin alley between their house—well, *Victoria's* house—and the next was paved with smooth stones that reminded Audrey of river rocks. Her boots clacked over them as she retreated from the home she shared with her best friend and headed into one of the city's dozens of markets. Maybe she could distract herself by window shopping. Even though she didn't really enjoy browsing, she could use the occasion to discover a new section of Fairhaven. She already knew Bertha's street and the entire route to Fyrn's house by heart, but there were plenty of markets closer to the palace that she hadn't yet wandered through.

With each step, the massive white palace in the center of town neared. She loved looking at the towering spires, especially the centermost one that climbed almost all the way to the largest of the magnificent glowing green crystals overhead.

As her feet carried her into the tourist district, she scanned the shops to learn more about this section of the city. The ogres had thinned out and there were only elves everywhere, both behind the cash registers and browsing the aisles. In this district, there didn't seem to be a single non-elfish creature. This shopping area wasn't as busy as Main Street, but plenty of people surrounded her. Most, however, gave her space. After all, she was a *human* in their midst. Dozens of almond-shaped eyes watched her from delicate faces with pointy ears, and many leaned to their neighbors to murmur as she passed.

Hmm. Perhaps she didn't want to be noticed after all.

A curve in the road led to a large open-air marketplace, tables having been set up on both sides of the thoroughfare. White cloth covered the shopkeepers and their wares, and the tables displayed everything from folded suits to umbrellas and knickknacks. Audrey's eyes began to ache from moving constantly as she scanned every table, relishing the distraction.

Something glittering on a nearby stand caught her attention. The table was covered with carved crystals. She recognized a few of the statues—a cat and a small mouse— but many were mighty animals she hadn't seen before, immortalized in formidable poses with raised claws and bared fangs.

Beside the crystal figurines were four statues carved from some kind of white stone: a koi, a butterfly, a dolphin, and a dragon. Their eyes glimmered like tiny suns, full of fire. A ping in her chest urged her to pick them up and buy them all, whatever the cost.

For no logical reason, her instinct said these were special.

Audrey picked up the koi, and her fingers crackled with electricity when the cold stone met her skin. The figurine glowed as brilliantly as the center of a star. She jerked her hand back in surprise, dropping the small statue back onto the table, and the light show caught the clerk's attention.

The elf jogged over, his long black hair frizzy. "What did you do?"

"I don't know," Audrey said softly, mystified.

"You break it, you buy it. These aren't cheap, kid."

"What are they?"

He grinned, flashing a mischievous smile that reminded Audrey of a used car salesman's. "These are ancient relics from lost civilizations. You name the kingdom, and I guarantee I have something from it you can buy. But be warned—no one knows what magic each of these contains!"

She rolled her eyes. *Laying it on pretty thick there, aren't you, buddy?*

"Where are these from?" She pointed to the alabaster figurines.

"Ah, I'm not allowed to say." He winked.

She quirked an eyebrow, waiting in silence for him to get on with his sales pitch.

The shopkeeper picked up the koi, and Audrey suppressed the desire to pluck it from his hands. "The man who sold me these said I was never to tell anyone where I got them, but I will tell *you*, my dear, because I can see that you're special. They're from the one and only Atlantis."

Audrey frowned, astounded at his blatant showmanship. "Atlantis?"

"I can tell you don't believe me, but I assure you it's true."

"Uh-huh." Perhaps that was her cue to leave. This guy was obviously trying to pull the wool over her eyes, but she couldn't deny what she had seen. Carefully Audrey reached for the butterfly, curious to see what would happen if she touched a different figurine. As before, energy crackled through her body and the stone glowed.

Wait. Hold on.

She frowned, stepping away from the booth as a

thought occurred to her. *This was a parlor trick.* He must have enchanted them somehow to encourage fools to buy his wares. Without another word she disappeared back into the crowd, but the haunting tug continued to pull her toward the white stone trinkets.

They're special. She knew it with every fiber of her being even if she had no idea why or how.

Careful to stay out of sight, she ducked into an alley where she could watch the booth. As she stared at the trinkets, a jealous twinge told her to go buy them *now*, before anyone else had the chance. Body tense, she leaned against the wall and forced herself to wait.

An elvish woman in a brilliant purple gown paused by the stall, eyes on the figurines. The woman lifted the koi figurine, her dainty fingers exploring the statue's curves. Audrey bristled, suppressing the utterly irrational impulse to run over and buy the white stone carvings out from under her.

But nothing happened. The stone didn't glow. In fact, the brilliant fire to the crystal eyes faded almost completely.

Audrey perked up, curious about her discovery. The figurines had reacted to *her*.

Only to her.

To test her theory, she waited while four more elvish women and a rare ogre handled the figurines. Everyone seemed drawn to their elegance and beauty, but no one could make them glow like she had.

Sold.

Audrey returned to the booth and gestured to the figurines. "What are you asking for these?"

"Fifteen each. But for you, I can go as low as ten."

"Thirty for all four."

His eyebrows shot nearly into his hairline. "I would be taking a loss! I have a family to feed, and—"

"I think we both know that's not true."

He smirked, his offended expression dissolving in an instant. "Clever girl. Fine. You have yourself a deal."

Audrey nodded, setting her hands on her hips as he wrapped each of them in paper for her. She could feel that these were magical. Part of her worried that they reacted only to humans, but she doubted it. There was magic in these figurines, and she would learn everything she could about them.

Deep down, she hoped this confirmed what she had desperately wished for: that, like Victoria, Audrey had her own brand of magic. Perhaps one only *she* could use.

CHAPTER THREE

Sitting in his office, Fyrn pushed aside yet another envelope with the United States government seal across the back. He had received a dozen of these in the last few months, all with the same request: *Come to Washington.*

The Order of the Silver Griffins might have excommunicated him for the snafu that gave Victoria's parents the means to blackmail him, but the human governments still reached out to him regularly. They didn't care if he didn't have a shiny badge anymore. As long as he could do for them what they needed done and took care of the magical creatures that threatened their cities, they called on him and paid him well for it. In fact, they had bankrolled several of his private projects without even knowing it. Their money kept him afloat.

But Fyrn had a more important project now: Victoria.

He couldn't deny the truth. Victoria would be massacred in a fight with Luak if she didn't get stronger. She could now produce and wield either the shield or the sword, but not both at the same time. If she were to succeed in a real fight—especially against someone as experienced as Luak—she would need both, as well as her magical ability to heal the blows she inevitably would take.

No matter how hard she trained or for how long, human bodies had limitations below what was required to master this particular Rhazdon Artifact. She was pushing her physical limits already.

She wouldn't be able to do it... not without help.

Fyrn had mastered more spells during his early schooling than most wizards mastered in their entire lives, but even he didn't know of any spells that could give Victoria as much strength she would need. He had spent days poring over the hundreds and hundreds of books in his collection. He had even inquired of some of his wizard contacts who still spoke to him, and though he never told them the full story, no one had an answer.

This Rhazdon Artifact had been made for an Oriceran being, something she wasn't and never could be. No spell could help her, and Fyrn was out of ideas.

Well, that wasn't entirely true. He had one idea—one Victoria herself had given him.

Find another Rhazdon Artifact.

He pushed himself to his feet and paced his study in an endless circle. What a horrible idea. He shouldn't even be considering giving her another Rhazdon Artifact, much less thinking about which one she should look for. It was a terrible idea, one he could never condone.

... and yet here he was.

Rhazdon Artifact, or failure. Those appeared to be her only options.

"*Videtur*," he said to the air.

Quick as a whip, one of his fairy spies appeared in the doorway. She was never far from him, and their magic word allowed him to summon her regardless of where she was. The beautiful fairy's red hair spiraled around her tiny face, nearly as long as her body. With her blue eyes focused on him, she wrung her hands with concern. "Yes, sir? Are you all right?"

"I am. I need you to find a particular Rhazdon Artifact."

She gasped, tiny hands covering her red lips. Her surprise lasted only a second, however, and she quickly nodded. "After everything you've done for us, we'll do anything for you, sir. You know that."

Fyrn nodded. "I do. It's an onyx bear figurine. Look everywhere."

"It will take me quite a while, sir. I'll have to make new contacts."

"Do what you must, but find out where it is. Don't retrieve it yourself, do you understand?"

She nodded. "Will it kill me if I try?"

"Most likely. Don't get hurt, little one."

"Yes, sir." Her gossamer wings beat the air and turned her toward the door.

"And Melzzie?"

She paused, hovering in the air as she peered over her tiny shoulder.

"Thank you," Fyrn said.

A thin smile crossed her lips. She nodded and whizzed off on her errand as quickly as she had come. His fairies had their own access doors to the house, which let them in and out even when he wasn't home. After all they had done for him through the decades, he knew they and they alone could be trusted with that sort of access.

He slumped in his chair, rubbing his temples as he stared at the mess of parchments on his desk. He had kept so much from her about Luak, about all the other people the monster had killed. But it was time. This would be one of her final tests: did she have a good heart, or would she be consumed by bloodlust?

In his soul, Fyrn knew she had the capacity for greatness. Not just because she was headstrong and determined, but because she was kind. She'd shown compassion when most hosts would have surrendered to greed.

But would it last?

CHAPTER FOUR

A week after she had found the alabaster figurines, Audrey lay in her bed with the door closed. On any other day Audrey would have been in the basement playing with her new gym, working out on the punching bag or practicing her sword techniques in the mirrored arena, but today she was curled up in her blanket with her chin on her pillow as she lifted a glowing white prism in her hands.

It was the latest of her finds, and by far her favorite. Though it hadn't been carved into a fun shape, it glowed brighter than the others when she held it. This one had more power, though she didn't understand how she knew that. Palm flat, joyful anticipation swirling in her chest, Audrey watched in awe as the crystal hovered above her skin, beautiful and glowing, filled with a magic she didn't understand.

But she wanted to.

The other four figurines she had bought from the shop-keeper sat in the bedside table drawer beside her. Each had its own cushion, a place of prominence. She didn't know why, but her instinct warned her to treat them with respect. They were special. Powerful.

They were hers.

True, she had used Victoria's money to buy them, but at least she had haggled. It wasn't like she had a job anyway. Victoria had said her money was Audrey's, but it still felt very much like Victoria's. In a way, buying anything for herself felt like stealing from her friend, even though Victoria had insisted Audrey quit working at Bertha's and just enjoy herself.

And yet, every denni she spent generated a twinge of guilt.

Still in her pajamas at two in the afternoon, Audrey pushed the thought aside and stood, the crystal hovering above her palm. It was time for an experiment, one she didn't fully want to run because she wasn't sure if she would like what she discovered.

Time to see if these crystals only responded to her, or to any human.

She hurried down the stairs and placed her beautiful prism in the middle of the kitchen table. She hesitated, unwilling at first to let it go, but she finally forced herself to set it down. She had to know if she was special.

An irrational voice in her head told her to grab it, to hoard it, to make sure no one took it from her, but she swallowed hard and turned her back on the stone.

"Victoria!" she shouted into the house.

"What?" Victoria shouted back, her voice distant. She was in the basement. Sure enough, the smack of a fist hitting the punching bag followed Victoria's voice, as well as the rattle of chains as the bag swung.

"Come here. Let's talk about dinner." Audrey slammed a cabinet door to emphasize her point.

Audrey didn't care about dinner. It was an excuse to get her friend up here without her knowing why. To see if Victoria was drawn to the crystal too. More importantly, Audrey needed to know what happened when Victoria touched it.

The heavy thud of feet on the stairs set Audrey's pulse racing with nerves and anticipation. To be innocuous, Audrey knelt to rifle through one of the cabinets without even remembering what was in this particular one. Pans, from the look of it, and a couple pots with lids.

The door to the basement swung open, and the kitchen floor creaked. A chair scraped along the floor and Victoria, breathing heavily, slumped into the seat. "I would kill for a potpie. Why don't we eat out tonight? Let's go see Bertha and ask her to cook us something delicious."

Audrey forced a smile and stood. "Works for me."

"Hey, what's this?" Victoria leaned over the table, reaching for the prism.

Every fiber of Audrey's being screamed for her to grab it from underneath Victoria's hand. Her very soul reached for it, but Audrey forced herself to remain still. She didn't like the effect the carvings had on her, but she couldn't deny their power or how they made her feel. *Special.* Part of her didn't want to lose that sense of uniqueness. She didn't want to discover that just *any* human had an impact on them. She wanted to believe that only she could make them come to life, but it wasn't enough to believe. She had to *know*.

Victoria lifted the prism into her hand, smiling as she

studied it. Light refracted from its faceted edges, but it didn't glow.

As with the elves in the marketplace, the crystal did nothing when someone else touched it.

Audrey smiled. She couldn't help it. Gratitude and joy buzzed through her. "I found that in a new marketplace. Pretty, isn't it?"

"Yeah, it really is. Is this the new centerpiece for the table?"

Audrey shook her head. "I was playing with it when I thought about food. I'll go put it back in my room."

"Huh. Cool." Victoria set it back on the table without hesitation. The crystal didn't call to Victoria the way it called to Audrey, and a realization burned within Audrey like fire. *She had her own brand of magic.*

After a lifetime of playing second fiddle to her best friend, Audrey was finally special. Whatever these crystals were, they held secrets that only she could unravel.

Victoria stood and walked toward her room at the back of the townhouse's first floor. "I need to clean up, so let's head out in about ten or fifteen minutes. Sound good?"

"Works for me." Once Victoria was out of sight, Audrey grabbed the crystal and trotted up the stairs to her room. The crystal hummed, glimmering at her touch. She shut the door behind her and fell with a happy sigh onto her bed, beaming as she studied it. It still glowed in her hands, ripples of light shimmering through it like waves in an ocean.

"What are you?" she asked the crystal.

It pulsed, the light within moving to a beat she couldn't hear. The pulsing light sped up, and Audrey felt a burst of energy within her. It felt like a sugar rush, but it was far stronger. She wanted to dance, sing, holler—anything to expend this overwhelming energy rushing through her.

White light sparked where her fingertip met the crystal. There was a sizzling sound, and smoke rose from her fingers.

She gasped and dropped the crystal on the bed. The glow faded, as did the overwhelming energy. Chest heaving with surprise, Audrey set a hand on her heart in a half-assed attempt to calm herself. She stared at the crystal, bewildered.

Something deep in her core warned her to tell no one. Though she didn't believe they were from Atlantis, she had a nagging feeling that those who did know what these stones really were would kill to take them from her. Whatever they were, they did more than just glow. They had real power. Real magic.

And they belonged to *her*.

CHAPTER FIVE

Showered and refreshed after her workout, Victoria led
Audrey to Bertha's down a remarkably empty street.
Styx hovered, aimlessly flying from side to side as he
scanned the road ahead. Every now and then an ogre or an
elf walked by, and every single one cast her a wary glance.
With each step, Victoria became more nervous and aware
that something was wrong.

The problem was, she didn't know *what* was wrong. It
was setting her nerves on fire.

"You feel that?" Audrey reached for the sword at her
side, lifting the hilt an inch or two as she surveyed the
empty street.

"I feel like we're walking into a trap," Victoria said. She
summoned her shield, and the heavy weight in her palm
made her feel safer. She scanned every single window and
her eyes hesitated on every shadow, but she saw no one.
Not even a curtain moved in the silent Fairhaven evening.

They waited for several minutes. Victoria was certain
that something or someone would jump out and attack

them at any moment. Her grip tightened on the shield's handle and her shoulders tensed as she waited for a fight.

It never came.

Victoria slammed her fist against Bertha's front door, Audrey keeping watch over the fairly empty street behind her. Styx mimicked Victoria, banging his tiny fist on the storefront. Save for the occasional ogre stomping toward one of the shops, they seemed to be alone on what was supposed to be the busiest street in town.

The door creaked open a crack to reveal two giant eyes. Bertha grumbled, "No need to be banging on my door. A simple knock would have done."

Victoria crossed her arms. "You're closed, Bertha. You're *never* closed during the day."

Bertha sighed deeply, her eyes roaming over the street, and gestured for them to come in. "Quietly, now."

They hurried inside and Bertha closed the door as quickly as she could, then pressed her back against it and looked at them both. "I didn't want to interrupt your training, Victoria, and I wasn't expecting Audrey until I train with her tomorrow, but something has happened. Something bad."

With Styx on her shoulder, Victoria peeked out the front window as an elf in a long red cloak hurried by. The woman lifted the hood over her head, peeking around the side of it as though she were checking to see if she was being followed. A strand of long blonde hair escaped the hood as she picked up the pace, disappearing beyond the scope of the window.

"What's happening?" Audrey set her hands on her hips.

Bertha lumbered toward the back of her house, floor creaking under her every step. "Come."

"Tell us what's going on, Bertha." Victoria followed closely, and the subtle tap of Audrey's boots against the hardwood planks meant she was behind them as they neared the back of the house.

Bertha peeked out the glass panes in the back door. "There's been more crime lately. Disappearances. Even a few murders, I've been told. They seem to have been hushed up, but the king won't leave his castle. He only makes appearances on his balcony. That means danger, girls. There's something dark in Fairhaven, and if the king is afraid then we all should be, because he will not protect us."

Victoria squared her shoulders and cast a wary look at Audrey. Arms crossed, Audrey stared at the floor, the slight indent in her cheek an indicator that she was lost in thought.

Victoria paced the kitchen. "What could it be?"

"And who was murdered?" Audrey slumped into the chair at the head of the table.

"There are those who believe the snarx was only the beginning," Bertha said, grabbing a random bowl off the counter and stirring. She didn't even look into it, so Victoria wondered if the ogre was stress-cooking.

Victoria paused her pacing. "What do you mean?"

"We know that Luak riled the snarx into a frenzy, forcing it to attack us, but some believe there are more monsters where the snarx came from. Maybe he let all sorts of creatures loose in the bowels of Fairhaven, creatures which are getting hungry now that he has left the city. Without him to keep them in check, they're getting braver. They're in our streets."

"Has anyone seen them?"

Bertha shook her head. "Just the corpses. And they've heard the screams. Whatever is hunting here is quick, silent, and deadly. I've never seen anything like it."

Styx squeaked with horror, and Victoria nearly did the same. This sounded bad.

"You know, a grate on all the tunnels would solve these monster problems," Audrey muttered under her breath.

Bertha opened her mouth to speak, but shut it almost as quickly. She rubbed her chin with her hand. "That's actually a marvelous idea."

Audrey massaged her temples. Anyone else would simply see a tired girl. Victoria knew the gesture meant, "You fucking morons."

Victoria cleared her throat and leaned against a chair for support. "We have to do something."

To her credit, Audrey didn't make a peep. She stared at the table, one hand in her pocket. A gentle glow radiated through the fabric.

"What—" Victoria squinted at Audrey's pants, wondering if her eyes were playing tricks on her.

Audrey snapped her head up, eyes shifting back into focus as she followed Victoria's line of sight. She pulled her hand out of her pocket and the glow faded. "You're right, Victoria. We need to do something."

Surprised, Victoria frowned. "Seriously? You agree?

What about the whole 'you don't owe this city shit' spiel you gave me last time?"

Audrey shrugged, arms crossed. "I was wrong. You already proved that to me."

Deep in Victoria's gut, a warning bell sounded. Something was off, and while Audrey wasn't necessarily lying, she was hiding something.

Something big.

An unfamiliar feeling hit Victoria hard in the chest, and she ached at the sensation. It was almost a sense of loss or betrayal, but through it all she felt sadness. In her quest to kill Luak and train as hard as possible so she could beat him, she had all but ignored Audrey.

It clicked for her: she *missed* Audrey. Aside from the occasional Berserk practice or rare time at the dinner table together, they didn't spend much time just hanging out anymore. In fact, the most time they had spent together lately was when they had killed the snarx.

Audrey had never kept anything from her before. They had told each other everything, but now it was clear that Audrey had a secret—something significant she felt she couldn't share. And that was wholly Victoria's fault. She had left Audrey pretty much alone.

The city might have needed Victoria's help, but she owed her friend more.

CHAPTER SIX

Audrey was careful to keep her eyes peeled on her way home. She had stayed behind to train with Bertha after Victoria headed back to the house to come up with a plan. While most of the city were scared of whatever darkness plagued them, Audrey and Victoria could handle themselves.

Grinning, Audrey fiddled with the magic stone in her pocket. She could definitely handle herself now that she had secret magic that could create sparks and feed her energy. Part of her ached to use it, even wished she would run into a creature so that she could discover the true capacity of these crystals' magic.

But she knew better. She shouldn't invite danger into her life just to play with power she didn't understand.

Aside from a few shifty glances from strangers she passed in the street, nothing notable happened on her way home. No attacks. No eerie sensations.

Bummer.

As she closed the front door behind her, the homey

aroma of cooking pasta captured her attention. She smiled and followed her nose into the kitchen, to find Victoria ferociously stirring a pot while Styx sat on the edge of the counter kicking his tiny legs.

Oh.

"You're stress-cooking," Audrey said.

Victoria laughed. "What, I can't do something nice for my friend?"

Audrey crossed her arms and quirked an eyebrow, giving her friend a once-over. "I've known you since middle school. You only cook when you're stressed out about something. Spill."

Victoria's shoulders drooped, and she put a bowl filled with some kind of creamy sauce on the counter. "Just eat my food."

Audrey chuckled and sat at the table. "If you insist."

Victoria set a banquet on the table, everything from spaghetti and meatballs to a tray of dumplings. Starchy, carb-filled goodness.

Audrey grabbed two plates from the cupboard. "Oh man, V. Are you trying to make me fat?"

Victoria chuckled. "Maybe."

With no one to bother them and the evening to themselves, they tucked into the feast. Audrey lost count of how many dumplings she ate. Each one tasted better than the last. "How can you be so good at making food when you only stress-cook?"

"I'm going to let you figure that one out, genius."

Audrey laughed. "Well, let's not think about stressful things."

Victoria chewed slowly on one of the dumplings and leaned back in her chair. "That rules out Fyrn."

"Yeah, no kidding. If he ever smiled, I'd check to see if someone was wearing a Fyrn mask."

Victoria laughed. "He's better than Diesel. My God, that wizard is insufferable."

"Because he's arrogant, or because he thinks you're soul mates?"

"Yes."

Audrey laughed and batted her eyes, doing her best to imitate Diesel's baritone. "Victoria, my truest *amour*, if I badger you enough perhaps I'll wear down your defenses and you'll fall madly in love with me!"

Victoria threw a piece of spaghetti at Audrey's head. Audrey tried to catch it in her mouth, but the noodle splatted on her face. They chuckled.

Audrey reached for another dumpling, even though her stomach felt as though it would explode. "These things are addictive."

"No kidding. Bertha taught me the recipe and I can't stop making them." Victoria popped another in her mouth.

"If we're too fat to protect Fairhaven, it's her fault."

"Basically."

The girls lounged in their seats, arms draped over the armrests and feet resting on the other chairs around the table.

Audrey resisted the impulse to grab another dumpling, mostly because it would require moving. "So, say we kill Luak. It's done. We're free from the need for revenge, and Fairhaven's free from his control. What's next?"

"For you? You should go home to your family and go to

college. I'll give you my fortune. You go start the next big company that sells for billions."

Audrey laughed. "As fun as that sounds, we've been over this. I'm not leaving you, Victoria."

A thin smile crept onto Victoria's face, and it warmed Audrey's heart. It was thanks enough. Victoria didn't have to say a thing.

"Well, if you stay here with me, at least we'll live comfortably." Victoria gestured to the grand house.

"Are you used to being rich yet?"

Victoria snorted. "Hell, yeah. I love it, but I won't forget where I came from. It's just a tool to make our lives easier."

"Much easier."

Victoria laughed and tossed a dumpling at Audrey this time, which she caught effortlessly in her mouth.

"What will *you* do?" Audrey prodded.

With a happy sigh, Victoria settled back in her chair. "Stay here. Take care of Fairhaven. Maybe usurp the throne."

Audrey laughed. "The important thing is to set achievable goals."

They chuckled, and in that moment everything was perfect. It was like when they had gotten together in Victoria's empty house for sleepovers while her parents were on assignment. Just the two of them, and loads of food.

Those had been good times. Too bad Audrey had to ruin the mood. "Tell me why you're stressed, Victoria."

"I'm not—"

Audrey caught her friend's eye and quirked her brow, daring Victoria to finish the lie.

"Ugh. Yes, fine. I'm stressed out."

"That's understandable. But don't worry, we'll figure something out. We'll find whatever's attacking people—"

"It's not that," Victoria interrupted.

Audrey hesitated, squinting a bit in confusion. "So what's going on?"

Victoria bit her lip, shaking her head as she stared out the kitchen window. "A lot is going on. Too much. It's been two months since my parents died, and I'm no closer to killing Luak. I've been training hard, but my body can only take so much. I'm not strong enough to wield the Rhazdon Artifact as it should be used. Fyrn's looking for a spell that can make me stronger, but I'm not optimistic."

"Victoria, we'll figure it out."

Victoria sighed. "That's not even the worst part, Audrey."

Audrey waited for Victoria to continue, heart skipping beats as she nervously wondered what was coming next.

"I've been ignoring you," Victoria finally said.

"What?"

"Except for little moments here and there, I've completely ignored you lately, and I'm sorry. I've been so caught up in revenge and bloodlust that I haven't spent time with you. I'm gone every day, and Bertha works most of the time. She can't train you constantly. You must be bored to tears."

Audrey was a bit confused. She didn't quite know how to take this. On one hand, Victoria was absolutely right. She *had* left Audrey to her own devices. On the other hand, the jealousy within Audrey burned brighter every day, and she wished with all her heart she could lock it away.

"I think you're being too hard on yourself," Audrey said.

"I don't," Victoria said softly.

Audrey laughed. "What on Earth has you feeling so guilty?"

Victoria studied Audrey for second, and the intensity made her squirm. It was like she knew something Audrey didn't—and Audrey didn't like that one bit.

"Do you still trust me?" Victoria eventually asked.

"Of course."

"Then why are you hiding something from me?"

If Audrey had been drinking something she would've spit it out from sheer surprise. Victoria knew. Somehow, someway, Victoria *knew*.

"Victoria... " Audrey didn't know what to say. She rubbed her neck, searching for the words to make this right.

Someone banged on the front door, and Audrey couldn't help but be grateful for the interruption. At first Victoria didn't budge. She didn't even look at the door, keeping the full weight of her gaze focused on Audrey.

"I'll get it," Audrey said. She hurried to the front door and swung it open, to find a small creature hovering in the doorway. It was no more than two inches tall, and looked like a very tiny human with long brown hair and rapidly humming wings that had faintly green coloration.

"I must speak with Victoria Brie at once," the fairy said, her voice high-pitched.

The tap of boots in the hallway meant Victoria had heard. Seconds later, she appeared beside Audrey and shook her head. "I'm a little busy."

"Fyrn needs to speak with you at once," the little fairy said.

"He can wait."

"Please, Miss Brie, I urge you to hurry. He said you will want to hear what he has to say."

Victoria sighed, one hand on her hip as she stared into the distance, no doubt weighing the pros and cons of interrupting the conversation she had started with Audrey. "Fine. Tell him I'm coming."

The fairy bowed and darted off. Victoria slammed the door and stared at Audrey.

To fill the silence, Audrey nodded toward the door. "Do you think he found the strength spell he was looking for?"

Victoria shrugged. "I doubt it. I don't mean to be pessimistic, but my gut says it's not possible."

Audrey ran her hand through her hair, unsure what to say. "Look, I don't... I'm not sure how to... "

Victoria lifted a graceful hand to silence Audrey and shook her head. "You don't have to tell me anything. That's what being friends is all about—you never *have* to do anything. At least not with me. I'm just... Well, Audrey, I'm hurt, that's all. I'm hurt that you don't trust me enough to tell me what's going on, but maybe I deserve it for not being here for you lately. But here's the thing: I will always be there for you: to help you, to listen, to give you whatever you need. I'm sorry if I've been a terrible friend."

With that Victoria opened the door and took off into the street, leaving the door ajar so as not to slam it in Audrey's face. Styx flew after her, moving so fast he was nothing but a white and brown blur. As Audrey watched her friend head toward Fyrn's house, she wondered if she was doing the right thing by keeping her new magic a secret. Victoria probably wouldn't be jealous. She would probably celebrate with Audrey, do everything she could to help Audrey learn to control this magic she channeled through the white stones.

But that deep, dark voice in Audrey's soul warned her to be silent. This was deadly magic, coveted magic, and all who knew of it were at risk.

CHAPTER SEVEN

About twenty minutes after the fairy left Victoria's door, Victoria sat in Fyrn's living room with a cup of tea in her hands. Apparently as confused as she, Styx sat on her shoulder and mimed drinking his own imaginary cup of tea each time she took an awkward sip.

Sitting in Fyrn's living room was freaking weird. He usually beat her with sticks and spells, so having him hand her a cup of tea told her that something was wrong.

Either he had been possessed by a very polite demon, or he was about to give her very bad news.

Time to get on with it. "What's going on, Fyrn?"

With a deep sigh, he sank into his armchair. "Luak has been murdering Rhazdon hosts. I know of eight confirmed kills, three of whom were Rhazdon hosts, and that's just in the last two months. I don't know what he was doing before he came after your parents, but I suspect he's been at this for a while. He's taking their Rhazdon Artifacts, and I don't know what he's doing with them."

Victoria gritted her teeth so hard pain shot up her jaw and down the back of her neck. The teacup trembled, but not from fear—she was seconds away from shattering it with her tightening grip.

Fyrn grabbed the cup, tea sloshing over the lip as he set it on the table. "Luak is not in Fairhaven. I suspect he's after yet another host. He's collecting Rhazdon Artifacts, Victoria, and that is very bad for you."

"Bad for me?! It's bad for the entire city. He wants Fairhaven, and if he has a lot of artifacts on his side I don't know how we're going to stop him!"

The barest hint of a smile played on Fyrn's lips, but Victoria didn't know what was funny. "This is serious, Fyrn! Are you laughing?"

He shook his head. "Not laughing. I'm merely impressed."

Victoria leaned back in her chair, shock overcoming her anger. "I don't think you've ever said those words to me before."

"Sure I have."

"Nope." She crossed her arms defiantly.

He shook his head. "Face it, Victoria. I just told you that your sworn enemy is amassing enough power to kill you, and the first thing you think of is protecting the city. That's not what most Rhazdon hosts would think."

"We've established that I'm not like most Rhazdon hosts."

"That you are not, Victoria."

She took a deep breath to settle her nerves and leaned her elbows on her knees. "So what's his plan? Amass enough power through the Rhazdon Artifacts to take over the city by force? Do you think the attacks and murders on the streets are his doing?"

Fyrn nodded. "He wants Fairhaven, there's no doubt about that. I absolutely believe the attacks in the streets are at least in part his responsibility, but I don't think he's acting alone. I think he's doing this on someone's orders."

"What makes you say that?"

"Before you faced the snarx, I received word that one of the Rhazdon Artifacts he took was a dragon amulet. This particular object is very obvious when it's attached to a body, but I did not see him wearing it when he tried to goad you into attacking him on the balcony after you killed the monster. This particular artifact is very powerful, and it would be very tempting for any Rhazdon host to wear."

"What does it do?"

Fyrn gave her a stern look over the bridge of his nose, and Victoria rolled her eyes. The look answered her question...she would never know.

"Therefore, it's safe to assume he's collecting Rhazdon Artifacts," Fyrn continued, taking control of the conversation once more.

She bit her lip. "Even worse, if you are right, he's collecting them for someone else. Someone strong enough to control him."

Fyrn nodded. "For the moment we need only worry about *him*. But in the future, I think we will face much stronger foes."

"Wonderful," Victoria said, slumping in her chair. With no room to sit on her shoulder anymore, Styx fluttered into the air and blew a raspberry at her.

Fyrn stroked his long white beard. "What I'm not

entirely sure I understand, though, is why he's going after Fairhaven only now."

"Why is he going after it at all?"

"Fairhaven is powerful, Victoria. The crystals surrounding the city have been thriving for tens of thousands of years without any influence from Oriceran at all. There is as much magic here as it is possible for a kemana to hold. It has massive reserves of energy, and it's only going to get stronger with time. I'm quite certain that whoever controls Fairhaven will become not just powerful, but immensely wealthy when Oriceran and Earth reconnect."

Victoria whistled. "I had no idea."

"When we treat a place as our home, it's easy to forget that others think of it as only a resource. People like Luak and whoever controls him don't care about the people who live here. They may not want anyone living here at all."

Victoria's hands balled into fists. "When will I be ready, Fyrn? I want this guy dead."

Fyrn shook his head. "I don't know, Victoria. I still don't have a solution for you. We need to make you stronger, and I'm not sure how to do that."

Victoria stood, furious. "I need some air. Anything else you want to tell me before I head home?"

He watched her for a moment, and Victoria wondered if he indeed had something else to say. After a few seconds, though, he leaned back in his chair and shook his head. "Good night, Victoria."

Anger and frustration still burning within her, she simply nodded and stormed out the front door into the cold night.

It took a lot to scare Fyrn Folly, but the rage and hatred in Victoria's eyes had left him speechless.

She had taken the news better than he thought she would, but those emotions concerned him. A small part of him feared she would not stay in control of the Rhazdon Artifact in her body, that she might indeed let the dark magic in her blood take over.

He stood and started pacing his living room as he debated his options. Of all the Rhazdon hosts he had ever met in his life, Victoria stood the greatest chance of living as normal a life as a Rhazdon host could. She came the closest to controlling the dark magic in her body, but she couldn't do it alone.

He snapped his fingers, an idea coming to him.

Audrey.

He needed to involve Audrey in Victoria's studies, use her friend to keep Victoria in line and remind Victoria of everything she was working toward. In cases like these—

A knock on the door interrupted his thoughts. He grumbled and gestured toward the door. It opened on command, but instead of a person he saw only a letter. A fox's tail disappeared into the brush, likely one of the emergency messengers who delivered important notices that needed immediate attention.

Fyrn picked up the letter and ripped it open. It was yet another handwritten note from one of his contacts in the American government. He groaned and tossed the letter onto his couch without bothering to finish it. He had more important things to tend to than some fetch quest for the CIA.

He shut the door and leaned against it, stroking his beard as his mind wandered. For the last decade he had been slowly building a very special project of his own. It had potential, but perhaps it was time to recruit the help of someone he trusted in order to finally complete it.

Victoria.

A pang in his heart warned him against trusting anyone besides his fairies. It had been quite a few decades since he had willingly divulged secrets. It was safest to keep his circle of trust small. The more who knew about his affairs and abilities, the more enemies he accumulated. It had always been that way. After all, Victoria could still lose herself to the power of the Rhazdon Artifact in her arm, and if she knew about his secret project she could destroy it. Or worse, use it to her advantage.

His was a lonely life, and he couldn't deny the sunshine Victoria brought into it. She was brilliant, learned what he taught almost as fast as he could impart it, and impressed him daily with her abilities. Even though he was a notorious grump, she could make him laugh. And most of all, the challenge of teaching a Rhazdon host to fight with honor and compassion was one of the greatest he had ever been given.

He cared about her. He cared if she died or failed in her attempts to protect Fairhaven. He didn't know what it was like to have a daughter, but he imagined this wasn't far from it.

So even if it cost him everything, he would trust her.

He sank to the floor, pain shooting down his leg as he tried to get comfortable. He would do everything in his power to save Victoria from being corrupted, but even a wizard as powerful as he could fail.

CHAPTER EIGHT

Victoria walked home from Berserk practice in silence, Audrey in step beside her while Styx flitted nearby. The unspoken tension between them said it all. They still hadn't finished the conversation during which Victoria had confronted Audrey about the secret she was keeping.

Everything was there, plain as day, yet Audrey still wouldn't tell her. It hurt Victoria more than any magical blast from Fyrn, or even a snarx bite.

A brunette fairy flitted up to them, the tiny creature hovering just in front of Victoria's face. "Fyrn would like to see you at once."

Victoria frowned. "It would be nice for him to come see me."

The fairy gestured to Audrey. "He would like your friend to accompany you. He has requested you both. Shall I tell him you're coming?"

Audrey quirked an eyebrow. "Why would he want to see me?"

The fairy shrugged her tiny shoulders. "He never tells me anything more than what message to deliver."

Victoria set her hands on her hips. "Let's go see what he wants."

As the fairy darted off, Victoria headed up the familiar trail to Fyrn's house. She kept her eyes peeled, never once allowing herself to relax in the empty streets. It was strange to see Fairhaven with barely a soul on the roads, but everyone was still terrified. Despite the year's Berserk season only just starting with the game the snarx had interrupted, none of the players would show up to compete. Even her Berserk team had decided to cancel their matches, much to her and Audrey's disappointment. Something silent and deadly was taking the city over, and even though she and Audrey weren't speaking much at the moment Victoria was grateful to have Audrey at her side.

When they finally reached the wizard's house, he was standing on the front stoop. He gestured with a finger and headed for the cave he and Victoria often used to reach the tunnels beneath the city.

"What's all this about, Fyrn?" Victoria asked.

"Victoria, I have to show you something. I believe you are ready for the next level of your studies. Both of you."

"Wait, me too?" Audrey asked.

Fyrn nodded. "I should've included you in the training from the beginning."

A subtle smile broke across Audrey's lips.

As they entered the cave, the crystal atop Fyrn's staff blazed to life and lit the way. Fyrn led them through the tunnels beneath Fairhaven for what felt like hours, and each cave they passed seemed darker than the one before.

"In here." After hours of silence, Fyrn led them through a tunnel into what had to be the darkest cave Victoria had ever seen. The pitch-black consumed her, weighing on her like a heavy blanket. The gentle tap of water hitting rock echoed forever, implying great height, and the rusty smell of moss filled her nose.

Fyrn muttered under his breath and tapped his staff once on the ground. Three ribbons of green light appeared around the crystal at the tip and with a burst of energy radiated in every direction, igniting little pockets of light along the rocky walls.

It was like seeing the night sky suddenly light up with little green stars.

Victoria could now tell that the cave was both massively deep and incredibly tall. Black water covered the entire floor, except for a stone walkway through the center of the cavern. Fyrn led them toward the darkness at the end of the path.

After about ten minutes of walking, they finally reached the end of the long tunnel. There, on a pedestal against the far wall, was a crystal easily as long and thick as Victoria's torso. Its tips were as sharp as daggers. Light radiated from within, as if there were a golden fog trapped inside it. The glow pulsed and pushed against the walls, eager to get out.

"Fyrn, what is this?" Victoria asked.

"A little while ago, Victoria, I told you the difference between relics and artifacts. Do you remember?"

She nodded. "A relic is like a battery, or an energy source. An artifact has incredible power, but you can't access that power without an energy source. The artifact is like a flashlight, and the relic would be like the battery used to power it."

Fyrn nodded. "Right. This crystal here is a relic, one of the largest on Earth. It contains immense stores of Oriceran magic."

"Wow," Audrey said, her voice almost a whisper as she reached out to touch it. The light within shifted, streaming toward her finger. It seemed to reach for her as much as she reached for it.

Before her finger touched the crystal, however, Fyrn smacked her hand with his staff.

She shook out her hand, grimacing. "Ow! What the hell?"

"You shouldn't touch ancient stores of magic, girl. This one is powerful enough to decimate several cities. And you were going to just touch it?"

"Sorry."

He sighed deeply. "I brought you here as a sign of faith. If I were to sell this I would become a billionaire overnight. It's immensely valuable, and if most people here knew of it they would kill me to get it. Do you understand?"

Victoria stood a bit taller, scared at the thought that something so valuable was stored in the tunnels beneath Fairhaven. "Why do you keep it here? It hardly seems secure enough. Why not put it in a bank vault?"

Fyrn laughed. "Vaults can be broken into. The enchantments I placed across this tunnel cannot be breached. You could enter because I invited you, but if you tried to come in without me you would be lost in an endless labyrinth of darkness. You would die of starvation, alone in the shadows."

"Fuck," Audrey said softly, hand on her heart.

"Why do you have this?" Victoria pointed to the relic.

Fyrn rested his weight on the walking stick, studying them both with an expression Victoria couldn't quite place. It seemed to be a combination of pride and concern. "I'm building a new kind of weapon."

"A weapon?" Victoria and Audrey asked in unison. Their voices echoed through the cave.

He nodded. "They're not done. Not close. But when I am finished, the weapons I'm building will be the true protectors of Fairhaven. None will dare harm us again, from within or without."

Victoria eyed the crystal hesitantly. "Fyrn, what if this falls into the wrong hands? This could be abused as easily as it can benefit us."

Fyrn's eyes crinkled, and a warm smile spread across his face. "As long as you remember to lead with compassion like that, I won't worry."

She smiled, a bit of gratitude snaking through her at his trust. "Thank you for sharing this with us. How can we help?"

"For now, you can keep this to yourselves. When the time comes, I may need help using the weapons."

"Can we see the other half? The artifact part?" Audrey gestured into the darkness as though something would appear suddenly from the shadows.

Fyrn shook his head. "I'll tell you more in due time. For now, appreciate that you are one of a select few who know that such power exists below Fairhaven as well as above it."

He headed for the exit, and Victoria marveled at their little field trip. She had a feeling this had been incredibly difficult for him, that it had required him to do what he hated most: trust someone else. It was the only reason she could think of for him to bring them down here. He wanted to share with them a project that could get him killed.

It clicked for her. She was his backup plan, his heir. If anything happened to him, he wanted her to finish his work. And she would, to the best of her ability, do everything she could to live up to the expectations he was placing on her.

With every step Audrey took on the way home, she nearly spilled the beans to Victoria.

Each was weighed with guilt that she would keep anything at all from Victoria, much less something as significant as hidden power. But that voice in the back of her mind was as loud as ever.

Tell no one.

Yeah, but it's Victoria.

Tell no one.

Victoria can be trusted.

Tell no one.

The voice was quiet but forceful, and the more Audrey heard it, the more she felt as though it wasn't her subconscious. She didn't know how else to describe it. It felt "other," like something outside her that was somehow also resonating deep in her chest.

"Victoria," Audrey finally said, breaking the spell of silence between them.

"Yeah?"

"There's something I have to tell you."

Victoria didn't respond. She simply waited, hands in her pockets, as they strolled home down a fairly empty road.

"I've... Well, you see, I've... "

Someone screamed, and Audrey's confession was frustratingly interrupted for the second time in a matter of days.

Victoria bolted toward the sound and Audrey followed closely. It was continuous, as though someone were screaming while running away from an attacker.

As they rounded the corner an elf ran toward them, slashes across the front of his ornate shirt. His wide eyes held a look of pure terror, and it was as though he couldn't even see them as he brushed past.

The ground rumbled. Victoria summoned her sword, and Audrey unsheathed hers. She also grabbed the white stone she now kept in her pocket at all times. Her favorite. The one that could summon sparks.

Perhaps a good helper here.

A shadow spread along the ground from around the corner of the house, followed seconds later by an ungodly creature. It towered over them, and the buildings beside it. Its massive claws dug into the ground, kicking up bricks and cobblestones with every step. Its dark blue skin glittered, suggesting scales, but it was the head that terrified Audrey the most. It was mostly mouth, with daggers for teeth and long spikes to protect the ears and neck.

It turned its head toward them and bared its teeth, hissing. Several clicks followed, like the sound of a lighter that wouldn't work.

"What the hell is that thing?" Audrey asked, taking a few steps back.

Victoria held her ground, sword raised and eyes narrowed on the creature. "I think this little guy is what's been plaguing our town."

"Little?"

It charged, feet scraping the ground and throwing dust and chunks of stone behind it as it dove for them.

Time to save the day—again.

Victoria attacked, and Audrey was right behind her. She scanned the creature for any sign of weakness, as Bertha had taught her to scan opponents. It swatted at them, the massive claws coming within inches of Audrey's face. Every time she got close, it swiped again or swung its tail at them.

They had to get it on its back.

"Attack the legs!" she shouted.

Victoria nodded and sliced into the nearest ankle. The creature screamed as its bright red blood spilled into the road, filling the gaps between the cobblestones like dry river channels after a dam broke.

Audrey attacked the creature's nearest leg, though her sword didn't go as deep as Victoria's magically sharp one. It stuck in the beast's skin, refusing to budge. The monster thrashed and its tail smacked Audrey hard in the chest. She flew backward and collided with a brick wall.

"Ow, fuck," she muttered, holding her head. Her ears rang, and she saw double. Her body ached and stung. She tried to stand, but she stumbled. Her palm hit the cold bricks of a nearby building, but the wall barely kept her upright.

The thing roared. Clicks followed.

"Audrey!" Victoria screamed.

Audrey spun to see the creature charging her, its teeth bared and its eyes focused on her torso. It was barely twenty feet from her and closing fast.

Head still spinning, she had only her instincts to protect her. She lifted one hand, her thin fingers the only thing between her and the beast, and grabbed the crystal in her pocket with the other, desperately wishing for a way out.

She needed a miracle.

A massive electric shock pulsed through her, skittering along her skin. Her hair floated around her head as though she were underwater, and her temples ached even more. Paralyzed, she could barely feel the pulsing sensations that had taken her over.

Tiny bursts of white light sped across her skin like cars on a highway and her hairs stood on end as the world around her began to go black. The blinding flare of white light reflected in the creature's gray eyes was the last thing she saw.

Victoria couldn't believe what she was seeing. Time slowed as she gaped.

White sparks covered Audrey's body. They raced along her skin until they blurred together into a seamless white glow. The creature froze, jaws wide and reaching for

Audrey's throat. It growled, no doubt frustrated that it couldn't move.

Audrey levitated slightly, her toes hovering above the cobblestones as her hair whipped around her face. Victoria couldn't even see her friend's eyes anymore—everything was lost in the brilliant white glow.

Sparks leapt from her skin and attacked the creature in front of her, and with every spark that landed the paralyzed creature screamed. Smoke began to rise from its skin, and the attacks from the sparks grew more frequent.

In a final violent blow, a bolt of white lightning shot from Audrey to the creature, striking it squarely in the face. It screamed, smoke billowing off it now, and fell to the ground with a lingering sigh.

But Audrey didn't stop.

Her head flew back, and the white glow began to recede. She still hovered above the ground, and her skin began to change. It took on a silver sheen, like scales. Her hair straightened and darkened until it was as black as night.

It was Audrey—her face, her hands, her nose—but also something else. It was as though something had taken over Audrey's body, Victoria wasn't about to let that something steal her friend from her.

"Let her go!" Victoria shouted, lifting her sword.

A hand grabbed her shoulder, and she nearly decapitated the person without looking. Fyrn stood behind her, one brow quirked as he watched Audrey float.

"Astonishing," he said.

"What's happening to her? She looks possessed!"

Fyrn shook his head. "Quite the contrary. She's waking up."

"What the fuck are you talking about? This is my friend, Fyrn! I need to know she's okay!"

"She'll be fine," he said.

"So what's—"

"It seems Audrey isn't entirely human, Victoria. Your friend has been hiding something about her heritage from us. Time to find out what it is."

Victoria gaped at Audrey as his words penetrated. She knew Audrey had been hiding something, but this was quite a secret to keep.

CHAPTER NINE

When Audrey woke up, her head hurt like hell.

She groaned, pressing her hand to her face as she tried to get her bearings. The world spun around her, and she couldn't really see. Something soft was beneath her and she balled it in her palm, savoring the warm soothing touch of this foreign fabric.

The pounding in her head began to slow, and after a while she was able to open her eyes. Three faces stared down at her.

She yelped, caught off-guard. It took a moment to recognize Bertha, Fyrn, and Victoria. Audrey looked around to find that she was in her room, lying on top of her bed.

"Tell us exactly what happened. Everything you remember," Fyrn said.

"What are you talking about? I don't even know what happened. Did we kill the creature?"

Victoria nodded, arms crossed. "It's apparently called a 'chezlewok,' like that Berserk team we played the other day, and yes, you did. By yourself. With magic. Care to share with the class how you managed to do that?"

Audrey shrugged and stared at her hands, suppressing the desire to reach into her pocket and grab the crystal. "I'm not sure."

Fyrn stared at her over the bridge of his nose. "Audrey, guessing games take time and patience, and I don't have either. If you don't tell us everything right now, we can't help you at all."

Victoria took a step closer. "Every time we tried to get close to you the white light would flare up again. It looked like you might take us out the same way you took out the creature. In the end we had to let you burn out before we could bring you back here. You nearly took out an entire block of homes. We're lucky no one was reported missing, and even luckier that you're not in jail right now. Both Fyrn and Bertha pulled some strings to keep you out of the dungeons, because right now people think you're a menace. Yeah, you killed the creature, but as far as they're concerned you just took its place."

"That's ridiculous!" Audrey said.

"I think so too, girl, but let's face the facts. You've been hiding something from me for a little while now. I had no idea you could use magic at all. It looks like you have the ability to use magic, but you haven't had the training, and that could be deadly. We saw you kill today. We're just lucky you didn't kill a citizen. Magic takes study and training to master, or you can hurt people. What the fuck were you thinking?"

Bertha wagged her finger near Audrey's nose. "We're

lucky you didn't kill Victoria. She was by your side the whole time, trying to get you down."

Audrey shoulders drooped, and she hugged her knees. "I'm sorry."

"Then tell us everything," Fyrn said again.

Audrey sighed and reached into her pocket to pull out the crystal. It glowed at her touch, and all three people in her room flinched at the light as it played on the wall. She set it on the bed, and the light disappeared as soon as her skin left the crystal surface.

"But that's... " Victoria stared at the crystal with an expression of recognition.

Audrey nodded. "It's the crystal I put on the table the other night. I wanted to see how you reacted to it but didn't want you to know what it could do. I really wanted to study it, to understand it, but I still have no idea what this is. As far as I can tell, it only reacts to me."

Victoria frowned, and Audrey couldn't suppress the guilt that rose up like vomit in her throat. She had treated her best friend like a case study, all without telling her the truth.

"Victoria, I'm sorry."

Victoria looked away. "I know."

Fyrn lifted the crystal, and it was almost as though the energy faded from it with his touch. It seemed to go dead and hollow, and Audrey suppressed the impulse to grab it out of his palm. The wizard stroked his beard as he studied the item. "This is Atlantean."

Victoria scoffed. "As in Atlantis?"

Fyrn nodded.

"But that's just a myth!" Bertha said.

Audrey's mouth fell open. "Oh, shit."

All three of her visitors stared at her.

She stammered, "T-the shopkeeper told me it was from Atlantis, but I thought he was full of it. You know, acting like a showman to make me think it's more special than it is. But Atlantis is real?"

"Very." Fyrn set the crystal back on the bed, and Audrey lifted it into her palm. Bertha and Victoria objected at once, both reaching for the crystal that had lit up with Audrey's touch.

Victoria grabbed it and set it on the bed again. "Maybe you shouldn't touch that until we know more about it. Let's not blow up any more buildings today."

Audrey chuckled. "Suit yourself."

Fyrn stared at Audrey intently. "Do you understand what it means for an Atlantean object to react only to you?"

Audrey shrugged. "Not really. I'm human, same as Victoria. I don't know why it likes me."

"You're part Atlantean, Audrey," Fyrn said slowly.

Audrey just stared at him, not fully able to process what he was saying. It didn't make a lick of sense, especially given that Audrey had grown up a few doors from Victoria. Her parents had never said or done anything magical, much less owned a crystal. It wasn't possible for her to have magic in her blood. "I think you're mistaken, Fyrn."

"Far from it. Have you felt a change in yourself lately? Feelings of jealousy? Selfishness? Greed?"

Audrey sat up a little taller, stuttering as she protested without managing to get any of the words out. She glanced at Victoria and quickly looked away, once more shoving her emotions deep into her core.

Fyrn nodded. "This could've been much worse. Audrey, most people believe Atlantis is a lost civilization because Atlanteans *want* the public to believe that. The truth is, they simply don't want to be found. Atlanteans keep to themselves. There are two factions: those on Earth, and those in Oriceran. They have evolved over time to look starkly different, but they still respect each other all the same because to an Atlantean, other Atlanteans are superior than all other beings. There are very specific personality traits present in nearly every single member of their race."

Jealousy. Selfishness. Greed. Audrey had become intimately familiar with each of them.

Fyrn began to pace the room. "You hid this from us, and that was the worst possible thing you could have done. You could have destroyed everything Victoria has built and done so far with a single action."

"How on Earth could I—"

"If Fairhaven turned against you, what side would Victoria take?" Fyrn glared at Audrey, waiting for her to answer.

She didn't.

"I'd take your side, Audrey, no matter what," Victoria said softly.

Audrey sighed, disgusted with herself.

Fyrn nodded. "Audrey, it's evident that you have immense power within you. Unless you hone and train it, it's going to destroy not just others but you as well."

"At least I'm a *little* special," she snapped. As quickly as she spoke, she clapped her hand over her mouth and looked at Victoria.

To her credit, Victoria didn't look offended or hurt in any way. She looked sad. "Of course you're special, Audrey. You've always been special to me, dear. Priceless, and I'm sorry if I never let you know that."

Audrey opened her mouth to respond, but she couldn't form any words. She didn't know what to say. The anger and resentment still bubbled within her, churning in her chest like a deadly undertow in an ocean.

"Until we get this sorted out, there will be ground rules," Fyrn said, stroking his chin.

Audrey narrowed her eyes suspiciously. "Like what?"

"First of all, no Berserk games until this is dealt with."

"Not fair! I—"

"This is not a discussion!" Fyrn's voice thundered through the room, impossibly loud.

Audrey sank back against the headboard, mouth shutting with an audible click.

"Secondly," Fyrn continued, "you'll need training, but I'm afraid I'm unfamiliar with Atlantean culture and magic. I haven't met enough of them in my life to be of much help to you. I knew of one back when I was in the Order of the Silver Griffins, but we don't speak anymore. That means we're going to need to find you a proper mentor, Audrey. I'm afraid there's not much I can teach you, at least to start. We have to find you someone who can teach you to control this magic, wield it, and direct it in a constructive way."

"You mean—"

Fyrn nodded. "We must leave Fairhaven for a time and, by some miracle, find an Atlantean willing to train you."

"But how?"

Fyrn squeezed his eyes shut and pinched the brim of his

nose. "Don't concern yourself with the 'how.' For now, just heal. Victoria and I will take care of this."

Victoria perked up, eyebrow quirking as she studied the old wizard. He walked toward the door and gestured for her to join him, but she remained at the foot of the bed for a moment, gazing at Audrey.

"I'm with you, Audrey. To the end," Victoria said softly before following Fyrn out the door.

Audrey tried to stand and follow, but her legs were like jelly. They screamed at her to lie down again, and she obeyed. She could only watch as her best friend retreated into the hallway to save her yet again.

"I'm sorry," Audrey said, too softly for anyone to hear.

"There, there." Bertha patted Audrey's shoulder. It ached when the ogre's heavy hand pressed down on the tender muscle.

"Ow!"

"I will mix up an herbal compress for you. Back in a few." The ogre lumbered out of the room, and all was still and quiet.

Audrey stared at the crystal on the bedspread in front of her. She hadn't told them about the soft voice urging her to be silent, but she assumed that was the greed. She stared at her hands, wondering what it even meant to be part Atlantean. If Fyrn was right—and honestly, she doubted his theory—Audrey was partly a magical creature from an ancient and mostly secretive civilization. It sounded impossible, and yet she could control a brand of magic no one else could use.

She *was* special.

Despite the destruction she had caused, Audrey smiled.

She had a gift. She had an entire culture to discover. But most of all, she had *power*.

The memory of the sadness in Victoria's eyes snapped Audrey out of her daze. She lay on the bed, exhausted and aching, wondering what on earth she had gotten herself—and Victoria—into.

CHAPTER TEN

Victoria followed Fyrn closely as he led her down a dark alleyway in a seedy corner of Fairhaven. These streets reminded her of the first time Fyrn had come to her defense, all those weeks ago. An elf had attacked her in the street because he knew she was a Rhazdon host. Now that she had been exposed to the whole city as a Rhazdon host, she didn't have to worry about being recognized. Still, the seedy back streets made Victoria nervous, and she couldn't wait to leave.

She wondered what on Earth she and Fyrn were there for.

"There is something you need to know," Fyrn said, eyes scanning every alley they passed. So far they were alone, but Victoria had the feeling that wouldn't last.

"What is it?"

Fyrn hesitated. "I meant what I said about Atlanteans having specific personality traits. You need to be careful. Even though Audrey is your friend, the more she learns about her Atlantean heritage, the less like herself she will become. The more she reconnects with what she really is, the more careful you will need to be."

Victoria shook her head. "You don't know Audrey like I do. We've had disagreements and she's said mean shit about me before, but we always get over it in the end. We always make up."

"You don't understand," Fyrn said. He paused, turning on his heel so that Victoria had no choice but look him dead in the eye. "Audrey doesn't have control over this part of herself. The more Atlantean magic she touches, the more she will have to choose between being the person you know and surrendering herself to the Atlantean voice in her head. I haven't seen that many human hybrids of any race, much less Atlantean, but the magical side of them has always won in the end. This is bad news, Victoria. Very bad."

It took a moment for Victoria to understand the expression on his face—deep concern. Maybe even fear. He was legitimately worried, and that shook Victoria's confidence, however slightly.

But in the end, this was *Audrey*. In middle school, Audrey had bitch-slapped the school's Queen Bee at lunch to protect Victoria. In high school, she had pantsed a jock who had publicly shamed Victoria for having a crush on him. No one had dared fuck with Victoria, because in the end they hadn't dared fuck with Audrey.

When push came to shove, Audrey always chose Victoria. Audrey would never let her down.

When Victoria didn't respond, Fyrn mumbled something unintelligible and started searching the alleyways again. They passed a few crumbling brick ruins with boarded-up doors before Fyrn knocked his walking stick against a door with an ogre's head painted on it.

The ogre's head came to life, pivoting on an invisible neck to scan the empty street. It finally settled its gaze on Fyrn. "What's the password?"

Fyrn groaned and rubbed his face, cussing silently to himself.

"The password!" the ogre's head shouted.

"I'm a tense bastard and need to lighten up," Fyrn said through gritted teeth.

The ogre's head chuckled, bouncing a bit as it flashed a rotting smile. "Yeah, you do. Enter, Fyrn."

"Idiot thinks he's a damn comedian," Fyrn muttered under his breath. The door swung open, and he gestured for Victoria to follow him.

Somehow it was even darker inside the building than on the gloomy streets. The only light came from a few glowing lamps in the corners, which cast a dim glow over a floor littered with stained red and gold pillows. Every now and then she saw a body lying among the cushions, immobile and silent. Horrified, Victoria squinted to get a better look, but they were thankfully breathing.

The longer she looked, the more sprawled bodies she saw. A couple of beautiful elvish women stroked the hair of a man lying across their laps, his eyes glazed as he stared at the ceiling. If Victoria didn't know better she would think they were all high, but there weren't any hookahs or needles in sight.

"What is this place?" Victoria whispered to Fyrn.

Fyrn cast a weary glance at the person lying closest to

him. "In Fairhaven, we don't have heroin or cocaine. We have something deadlier."

He pointed to a young elf in the corner, who lifted one of the small crystals they used as currency in Fairhaven. He held it to the light, examining it and spinning it in his fingers for a moment before putting it into a small pipe and bringing the pipe to his lips. He inhaled, and the crystal glowed green. When he opened his eyes, the whites and irises and pupil had been replaced by a green glow.

Victoria jumped and stumbled backward, bumping into a support pillar. "But they're literally burning money! You use these crystals to buy things, and...they're smoking them?"

Fyrn nodded. "We use the denni for currency because they're powerful. People crave power, and the magic high this gives makes you feel immortal and important, as though the universe revolves around you. It's addictive, and only a fool would try this even once."

"Have you tried it?"

He chuckled. "Of course. Wizards go to college, too."

She frowned and scanned the faces on the floor. She recognized one of them, and it took a moment to realize she was mere feet away from the thief she had chased down on Main Street not too long ago. "Hey, that's the guy who keeps stealing shit around Bertha's shop."

"Stay focused, Victoria."

"Can't I punch him? Just a little bit."

Fyrn frowned, watching her as though he were testing her. "Victoria, come. We have a long night ahead of us."

Her jaw tightened. She longed to discuss it further, but

she obeyed. In the end, Audrey mattered more than some asshole thief in a drug den deep in the heart of Fairhaven.

At the end of the long row of pillows and bodies was a massive wooden door. Two ogres guarded it, arms crossed in front of their bodies in a way that reminded Victoria of the bouncers she had seen outside the Seattle clubs she had always wanted to go to. The ogres' beady eyes never left Victoria, and she tensed.

These fellas didn't look friendly.

As she neared, the taller one bent toward the doorknob and opened the door for them.

She gave him a sarcastic salute. "Thanks, buddy."

The ogre grunted in response.

Inside was a lavish office that contrasted starkly with the drug den out front. A mahogany desk sat in the middle of the room, with a luxurious red carpet beneath it and a roaring fireplace behind. Despite the fire the room seemed cool and comfortable, as though the heat couldn't reach them.

Victoria paused at the entry, feeling guilt at the thought of crossing such a beautiful floor in her filthy mud-covered boots. The office could have easily been in a mansion, and Victoria half-wondered if the door was a portal to another part of the world. The ornate office didn't match the drug den at all.

A short gnome-like creature sat in the chair, his seat raised so high that Victoria could see the leather cushion. He was dressed in a suit, and his ears poked out on either side of the chair. He was a small creature, maybe three feet tall, but something in his wicked sneer told Victoria she shouldn't mess with him.

"Welcome," he said, his voice grating like a file on metal. She flinched.

"I see you still haven't changed that password," Fyrn said with a frown.

The gremlin laughed. "I would think you'd enjoy having your own special password to speak to the most powerful gremlin in Fairhaven any time you wish. It's an honor."

"Uh huh." Fyrn quirked an eyebrow.

The gremlin set his fingertips together and leaned back in the chair. "So, old friend, I can only assume you need something. You never come to chat."

From the depths of his sleeves, Fyrn summoned a bag brimming with small crystals and threw it on the gremlin's desk. "I have questions, and I need answers."

The gremlin lazily glanced at the bag without reaching for it. "What sort of questions?"

"Very difficult ones to answer, Drefus."

The gremlin sighed and rubbed his ears, pulling on an earlobe. His ears fluttered like wings that wouldn't lift him. "You know I hate this vague shit you pull, Fyrn, but you do it every time. I'm not taking your money without knowing what you want. Give me details."

Fyrn hesitated, and Victoria studied the old wizard. His lips had tightened into a hard line, and he didn't flinch. He wasn't going to give in.

In the ensuing silence, Victoria glanced between Fyrn and the gremlin at the massive desk. This was a negotiation, apparently. Audrey had told her once that in business the first person to offer a price lost, but that didn't seem to be true in Fairhaven. Here information was more important, and Fyrn wanted a blanket agreement before he told the other a word of what he wanted.

Weird. Every time she thought she had started to understand this city, the situation changed and she learned something new that altered everything.

Drefus eventually laughed. "You certainly like playing hard to get, you old fart."

Fyrn shrugged, doing a great job of feigning indifference. "I'm overpaying you, frankly, for what I want to ask."

"I doubt that."

With a chuckle, Fyrn nodded to the bag of denni. "Is it a deal?"

The gremlin clicked his tongue in apparent disappointment and, without moving a muscle, shifted his gaze toward Victoria. "I want her."

"Absolutely not!" Fyrn's voice thundered in the office, shaking the very walls. The glass in a nearby window continued to rattle, and one of the ogre bodyguards had to set a hand on it to calm the tremor.

Instead of showing fear, the gremlin smiled. His eyes narrowed as if something in Fyrn's outburst had told him all he needed to know. "Now, hold on, Fyrn. Hear me out."

"There's nothing to hear. I don't barter lives. I have offered you more than enough money to cover what I need to know."

Drefus shook his head. "I don't need money. I have plenty. What I need is muscle, namely muscle the people fear. And she"—the gremlin nodded toward Victoria once more—"is a certified Rhazdon host. With her in my employ, my security detail would be complete."

"Your army, you mean," Fyrn said, scowling.

The gremlin chuckled. "You think so poorly of me, my friend."

Fyrn gestured to the bag of denni on the desk, and his hands glowed green. The bag lifted into the air and slowly floated back to him. "I think we're done."

Drefus set his index fingers on his nose, tapping them on the protuberance as he studied the wizard before him. "Fyrn, I must confess... Every time you come to me to ask for information or assistance, it's because you *need* it. I know for a fact that you cannot walk out of here, because you have no other way of getting what you need. You showed your cards, old man. You always do in the end."

"I'll go without if your price is Victoria."

The gremlin's eyes shifted to Victoria, and she tensed a bit under his gaze. He gave her a very slow onceover, the kind that made her feel as though she weren't wearing clothes. When guys did this to her at school she slapped them, but she probably wouldn't get away with that here. As his eyes roamed her, she felt like a piece of meat. Gritting her teeth, ready to attack this motherfucker even though she knew it was a bad idea, she set her hands on her hips and glared at him.

After what felt like an eternity he leaned forward and put his elbows on the desk, shoulders scrunching up by his ears. "Ask your question, and I will give you the price."

The wizard grabbed the bag of denni out of the air. "You can't have—"

"Yes, yes, Victoria is off limits. Fine. Ask."

Apparently backed into a corner, Fyrn complied. "I need the location of Atlantis."

The gremlin laughed. His shoulders shook, his ears

fluttered, and he held his head as though he had never heard anything funnier. "You never cease to amaze me, Fyrn. What trouble have you gotten yourself into now?"

"Never mind that. I need coordinates."

The laughter eventually died down, but he still wiped away a tear. "This won't be cheap."

"I figured."

"If you had come to anyone else, they would've told you it was impossible and laughed you out of the room. Anyone else would've thought you had finally gone insane and thrown you out, but I know more than most people. I can do better than coordinates. I can get you a map, complete with access passwords and hidden traps."

Fyrn scoffed. "Now I *know* you're lying. A full map? Where could you possibly have found one?"

"There are many people who owe me debts, and a certain treasure hunter I know took his sweet time repaying me. I made it a point to find him and ensure he gave me what was owed. He didn't have the money, but he did have a few interesting items on him. I, shall we say, *encouraged* him to part with them."

Victoria crossed her arms. "Did you kill him?"

The gremlin shifted his beady gaze to her and smiled. "Does it matter?"

"It does to me."

"Victoria, pick your battles," Fyrn said under his breath.

She hesitated, lifting her chin as she stared at the grinning crime boss in front of her. True, she didn't *know* he was a crime boss, but everything she had seen so far screamed magical mafia. The bodyguards. The drug den. The army. The hidden doorway to get in. He must have an empire to run. Her intuition warned her he and Fyrn weren't really friends, and she would be wise to treat him with caution.

Fyrn tapped his staff against the floor to recapture everyone's attention. "How do we know this map is legitimate? It could easily be a fake."

"Ordinarily I would agree, but he had in his possession several fascinating items that led me to believe he had actually been there. From our conversation it was clear he barely made it out with his life, and intended to return with an army. Unfortunately for him, he had debts to pay."

"What items?" Fyrn asked.

The gremlin snapped his fingers, and one of the masked guards by the door reached into a cabinet on the far wall. He pulled out a white stone, not unlike the one Audrey had hidden in her pocket. It was dead and lifeless in his hands, but Victoria imagined it would spring to life if Audrey touched it.

The gremlin grabbed the stone out of his minion's hands and tossed it between his palms. "I've managed to sell these to a few vendors around the city, and fools who like shiny things buy them. Few know that these are actually incredibly powerful artifacts. Look for yourself, Fyrn."

The gremlin chucked the white stone toward Fyrn, who caught it and studied its many facets. His thumb brushed something Victoria couldn't see, and he tilted it toward her. An ornate "A" had been carved on the largest facet, and the lines of the letter glowed as though it had iridescent ink embedded within it.

"Legitimate," Fyrn said.

Drefus nodded. "I had big plans for this map, Fyrn.

There are said to be riches unlike anything we've ever seen in the vaults of Atlantis, and as you've already mentioned, I have an army of my own. It wouldn't be easy or fun, but I *could* find this place. I could make a fortune. Why should I give this map to you for anything less than a Rhazdon host?"

"Because I'm not for sale," Victoria snapped.

"Pick your battles, little one." The gremlin echoed what Fyrn had said earlier, but his voice had dropped to a growl. It was a threat. A warning. She walked a line with every word she spoke, and it was clear this gremlin was powerful. He had wealth and muscle on his side.

But she had ancient dark magic in her blood. He had apparently forgotten she was more than an object to barter.

"Oh, I'm picking my battles quite carefully," she said, her voice sharp and fierce. She took a step forward, squaring her shoulders as she stared him down. "You can try to buy me, but even if you succeeded it would backfire. If you tried to control me even once, I would turn on you. I would break the things you love. I would destroy you and everything you have built from the inside out, and it would be easy for me. Effortless."

For full effect, she summoned her sword. The guards flinched and stepped backward, hands reaching for their own blades.

She grinned, narrowing her eyes and showing a bit of wicked glee. "You forget that I'm not an object. I'm not a toy. I'm a force to be reckoned with, and I will make your life a living hell if you fuck with me."

To his credit, Fyrn didn't say a word. Perhaps he was

picking his own battles as well, but he didn't interject and he didn't undermine her. She could see him in her peripheral vision, and he was as still as stone, his attention focused one hundred percent on the gremlin in the massive chair by the fireplace.

The gremlin leaned back, tapping his finger on his chin as he studied Victoria's face. "Very well. I have a new price, then. One that still involves you, but not in the way you expect."

She quirked an eyebrow without saying a thing, implying she was listening without indulging him further.

"You will owe me one favor, to be used at any time I wish. If you agree, I will give you the map." He snapped his fingers, and the guard who had originally retrieved the crystal now reached into a different cabinet and pulled out a scroll.

"Not a chance," Fyrn snapped.

Victoria hesitated. A favor didn't sound terrible.

"I won't go lower," the gremlin said, scowling. The wrinkles in his cheeks and forehead exaggerated the frown.

"You ask too much."

"Fine. I'll go to Atlantis myself, some other day." the crime boss gestured with his hand, and the thug to his left picked up the scroll and returned it to the cabinet.

Victoria nodded to the door. "Fyrn, can I have a word?"

"Victoria, don't—"

"A word, *please,*" she said with a glare.

He pursed his lips and grumbled, but begrudgingly gestured toward the door. Head held high, Victoria stepped into the hall with her mentor in tow. He slammed the door behind them and snapped his fingers. A yellow bubble popped to life around them, shimmering and glowing as though it were made of sunbeams.

"Wow, what's this?" she asked, pressing her finger against the bubble. Light rippled under her touch.

"A zone of silence. No one will hear us. More importantly, no one will hear me chew you out for undermining me in front of a crime boss. Victoria, never do that to me again, do you understand? Especially not in front of someone like him. It makes us look weak, and costs me my bargaining power."

"I didn't undermine you. I'm just asking you to reconsider your stance on this favor."

"We were not done negotiating."

"Are you sure about that? Because it looked like he put it away to me."

"He was bluffing."

"I don't think he was. He's come down pretty far in his bargaining already. I think this is the final offer." She set her hands on her hips and stared at Fyrn, daring him to disagree with her.

He didn't.

"It's too risky," the wizard eventually said.

She chewed on her lip, staring at the floor as her mind raced. "I don't feel like we have a choice."

"I hate it when you say that. There is always a choice."

She rolled her eyes. "Fine, let's look at our choices here. Choice number one is, we decline his offer and lose our chance at the map. What other way do we have to get her to Atlantis? How else can we help her find a mentor who can keep her from destroying herself and everyone around her?"

Fyrn stared at her for several moments, but she wasn't going to budge. Victoria would wait until he answered her, because she already knew what he would say.

"I don't know," Fyrn eventually admitted.

She nodded. "That's what I thought. Therefore, choice number two is, I agree to owe this man a favor. Why is that bad?"

Fyrn smacked the butt of his staff hard against the floor. "Do you know what kind of favors crime bosses ask for in Fairhaven?"

She shrugged. "Washing their cars?"

"Take this seriously!"

"Fine. I don't know, but I assume it'll be something seedy. Stealing, maybe."

"Try murder."

Her eyes went wide. Fyrn nodded. "You're powerful, Victoria, and I think sometimes you forget that. You forget what you can do. Even though you would never kill an innocent person, that doesn't mean someone won't manipulate you into it. That gremlin in there might look harmless to you, but he is bloodthirsty. I guarantee you the original owner of that map isn't breathing anymore, and he probably begged for death before Drefus was done with him. Not a kind man. This is not someone to whom you should owe anything, much less something as ill-defined as a favor."

A chill ran down Victoria's spine, and she stood straighter as she stared wide-eyed at her mentor. Fear rattled in her chest, but a simple fact remained. "If I say no to him, how will we get Audrey the help she needs?"

Fyrn sighed wearily and leaned on his staff, setting his forehead against the glowing orb on top. He seemed to lose himself in thought, his eyes twitching a bit as he no doubt racked his mind for an answer.

Several quiet minutes passed, filled with nothing but the sound of his breathing. The bubble must have also silenced the sounds coming into their space as well as those going out. She had never realized how much she enjoyed ambient noise until she was forced to listen to air shooting in and out her mentor's nose.

Bleck.

"Fyrn?" she eventually said.

He groaned and smacked his staff against the floor again in frustration. "I don't know, Victoria. I last met an Atlantean over fifty years ago, and I can guarantee you he's long dead. He was basically a walking skeleton when I met him, banished from the kingdom for a crime he would never share, and I haven't heard from him since. The salesperson who sold her those crystals didn't even know what they were, or he would've charged five to ten times more than he did. Every lead I have believes Atlantis is long gone, and all I have learned about the culture is what I've gathered from books. I have nothing to go on. I'm not qualified to teach her."

Victoria was in a bind, and she had to choose: owe this frightening creature a favor, or abandon her friend.

No contest.

She grimaced and chose her next words very, very carefully. "I understand the cost here. I understand what he's asking. But come on, Fyrn—you watched what happened today. She obliterated a massive creature I was having trouble handling by myself, and she made it look easy. What happens if we're not there to stop her next time? Or worse, what if we *can't?* If we don't help her learn to control herself, the next episode might be deadly. This guy wants a favor, and even a favor to a crime boss is a fair price to pay if it means I get to save my best friend. Don't fight me on this."

Fyrn rubbed his temples, shoulders drooping in defeat. "I wish I had an alternative. I don't like this at all."

"Neither do I."

"We should set limits on the favor. When you say yes, he's going to magically bind you to your word. Whatever he asks of you, you will be forced to do it. But if we set limits *before* he makes the request, *before* he binds you to the favor, we stand a chance of this not backfiring on us."

She nodded. "No killing."

"Agreed. No killing. No prolonged servitude on your part. One favor. And no betraying those you care for."

"Do you think that's enough?"

Fyrn shook his head. "It's the best we'll get."

Victoria tensed. With a tap of the staff against the floorboards the glowing bubble around them popped, and the moans and coughing from the drug den crashed into her like an ocean wave.

Fyrn gestured with his hand and the door opened on its own. Drefus was still sitting at his desk with his fingers pressed against each other, and he smirked as she entered.

He knew he had her. That bastard.

She squared her shoulders. "One favor, but there are rules."

The gremlin shook his head. "I don't do—"

"Rule number one," she interrupted, narrowing her eyes a bit for emphasis. "No killing."

The gremlin stiffened, pinning his ears against his head as he scowled. "I don't do—"

"Rule number two," she interrupted again, knowing she was testing her luck with this guy even though she had to. He needed to respect her. Anything less, and she risked him taking advantage of this favor. "No prolonged servitude on my part. You get one favor, and that's it."

The gremlin huffed and stood on his chair as he shoved his finger toward her. "Now see here—"

"Rule number three," she continued, her heart thudding in her chest at her own brazenness. "I will not betray those I love."

He stood as tall as a three-foot creature could in a cushioned chair, his shoulders squared as he all but growled at her, "Those are some restrictive demands."

"I'm sure you'll come up with some nefarious deed for me to do regardless."

Fyrn tensed beside her, but who was he kidding? They both knew the gremlin would abuse this favor to the best of his ability. She wasn't planting any ideas in his head. Might as well be honest about it.

A slow and wicked grin spread across the gremlin's face, and dread shot clear to Victoria's toes. It appeared he had already thought of the deed he wanted her to do, far faster than Victoria had anticipated.

"Very well, Victoria Brie, I accept your conditions." He

lifted his hand and a large gold coin appeared in his palm. He flipped it over in his fingers and held it out for her to grab.

She gave Fyrn a fleeting glance, and he nodded toward the coin. "Take it."

Victoria reached for the coin, never taking her eyes off the gremlin, and lifted it between her fingers. As soon as her skin touched it, she froze. It was as though her entire body had been encased in ice. A deep chill nibbled at every hair and pore on her body. She tried to break free, to summon her sword or do anything at all to protect herself, but she was utterly and completely immobile.

"I bind you to a favor based on the rules you provided: no killing, no prolonged servitude, and no betrayal of those you love. You're bound to this favor, and only when I return this coin will the spell be broken."

As quickly as it had come, the paralysis passed. The coin sprang from her hand and settled into the gremlin's open palm. He snickered as she sucked in several deep breaths and staggered backward, hand on her chest as she stared at the coin. He studied it, a worrisome smile still on his face, and gestured lazily to the thug behind him. The giant ogre grabbed the scroll from the chest once more and tossed it to Fyrn, who caught it effortlessly. He unrolled it, eyes darting over the parchment almost too quickly, and rolled it up once more. "Very good."

"Pleasure doing business with you, as always," Drefus said with a smirk.

Fyrn feigned a smile in response, but Victoria didn't bother with one at all. She watched the gremlin warily as they left, only taking her eyes off the crime boss when the door shut behind her.

"We should leave immediately, for *her* sake," Fyrn said, most likely referring to Audrey. They were no longer in their bubble of silence, and they would have to play the pronoun game until they were in a safe area again and could speak freely.

"How do we know that's real?" Victoria said with a nod to the scroll in his hand.

"It is," Fyrn said.

She shot him an incredulous look, but he gently shook his head. She was beginning to understand Fyrn's mannerisms, and this one seemed to mean, *Trust me.*

"Fine," Victoria said. Truth be told, she was grateful he had such concern for Audrey, but she knew in her heart he was more worried for the city. The power Audrey contained was not to be underestimated. It could kill hundreds, if not thousands, in one go. Hell, it almost *had.*

This wouldn't be fun.

CHAPTER ELEVEN

Later that evening, Fyrn slouched in his chair at home with the lights off. His mind buzzed with terrifying new fears. There was not only a Rhazdon host living in his home city, but also an untrained Atlantean with powerful magic that could kill half the populace in a single unrestrained moment.

But greater than his fear for his city was his fear for Victoria.

Victoria and Audrey had a connection, one no mortal could ever destroy. They were more than friends. They were sisters. Partners. He had seen it from the start, from the way they supported each other in their Berserk games to the way Audrey had sacrificed everything to protect Victoria against the snarx.

They relied on each other and trusted each other, but the Atlantean blood in Audrey's body would test their bond. As Audrey discovered her heritage and true nature, the Atlantean girl would either build Victoria to greater heights or destroy her completely.

They would either inspire each other to become the most powerful humans alive, or they would implode—together—and perhaps take Fairhaven with them.

The floorboards deep in the house creaked, and he sat at attention as his ears craned and twitched at the sounds. An elf's footsteps would be light as a feather, but this person slapped his shoes against the ground without caring whether anyone heard. The steps originated from the back of the house and were creeping toward the front, and a thin beam of light broke into the living room from the hallway.

Fyrn stood, shoving aside his concern for Victoria as bubbling anger at an intruder festered in his chest. He was in no mood to be merciful, and the thief would die.

As the burglar rounded the corner, Fyrn lifted his staff to attack. A beam of energy through the intruder's heart should do the trick.

But then the thief stepped into a ray of light coming through the window, and Fyrn recognized the suit.

He groaned and relaxed his shoulders, sighing a bit as he shook his head. The black suit and earpiece looked familiar—too familiar. It had to be a human from some sort of government agency. Fyrn had been ignoring summonses from the United States government for months, so apparently they had chosen another means to share their message.

Fyrn snapped his fingers and the lights in his home blazed to life. "Breaking into my house in the dark wearing a suit? I get that your superiors have a flare for drama, but this was a little unnecessary."

"We figured we needed to get your attention," the man said, turning off the flashlight with a flick of his thumb.

No longer in shadow, the man in the suit looked like every other man in a suit who had ever come to fetch him or greeted him on any of his government assignments. Same black cloth. Same short haircut. Same aviators tucked in the front pocket. Fyrn understood the need for a dress code, but this was just comical.

"The United States government needs your help, Mister Folly," the man in the suit said.

"I don't give a snarx' shit. Please leave my house."

The stranger shook his head. "You misunderstand. We are not *asking*."

Fyrn laughed. It began as a soft chuckle, but it grew until it shook his very shoulders. Imagine, a human government commanding a wizard as if he were at their beck and call! It was too ridiculous. He wiped a tear from his eye. "I can't tell you how much I needed that. *You*, commanding *me*? Do you want to die?"

"I would rather not," the man said, crossing his arms.

"Then get the fuck out of my house," Fyrn said, his smile dissolving.

"Look, Mister Folly, I'm going to be honest with you. I'm at the bottom of the totem pole. That's why I was chosen—if I died, no one would miss me. But if I *do* die, if I don't return and check-in, it's going to set into motion a certain series of events I can guarantee you don't want."

"Such as?"

"First you should know there is a rampaging creature tearing up the Seattle Underground, killing people and compromising the foundations of several buildings that are key to the city's history. We need a wizard we trust to handle this discreetly. My superiors have forgiven your past mistake, and they want you to help us with this problem."

"Why do you think I care? Honestly, get out before I throw you out. Final warning."

"Here's where the series of events comes into play. If you come with me, you'll be paid handsomely for your efforts. If you don't come with me to the surface tonight, certain information about the whereabouts of this city and its location might leak to the general American public. Certain videos of your past exploits. Certain filmed conversations we've had with you about certain creatures that aren't supposed to exist might find their way to the Web."

Fyrn's face burned with hatred. "Those were to never be recorded. How dare you threaten me!"

"I am deeply sorry, Mister Folly. It's not me, I promise. I'm a grunt. I came expecting to die tonight, to be perfectly honest, and I wouldn't blame you. But if you love this city and want to protect it from that kind of classified information getting out, you'll come with me."

Fyrn was tempted. He was deeply, painfully tempted to obliterate this man before him, but the temporary justice wouldn't be worth it in the end. He would need to have a talk with this man's superior, but for the moment his hands were tied.

"I have certain things to attend to before we leave," Fyrn said.

"I'll be happy to accompany you."

"You will stay here."

"But—"

"What am I going to do, disappear? You have my hands tied. Shut up, sit down, and wait until I return. And by God, don't touch anything. Melzzie!"

The fairy flitted into the living room, prompt as always. "Yes, sir?"

"Make sure he doesn't touch, read, or eat anything in my home. Zap him if you have to."

He had taught her how to channel her fairy magic into an electric attack, and the little fairy loved to zap anything and everything he would let her touch. She grinned and saluted. "Yes, sir!"

The man gaped for a moment before sitting down on the sofa. A cloud of dust rose around him, and he coughed.

Fyrn only had a few short hours to put everything in order for Victoria's trip before this government grunt got impatient and left without him. Stalling wouldn't work, and now Fyrn had no way of joining Victoria in Atlantis.

Time for Plan B.

He swallowed his pride and headed out the door, not altogether fond of what he was about to do.

CHAPTER TWELVE

"You're leaving? Is this a joke?" Victoria leaned both hands on her dining room table, bewildered by what Fyrn had just said.

"My hands are tied, Victoria. My choices are to let the American government expose Fairhaven or run their little errand for them."

"So we wait for you to come back, or better yet, let me help you. I want to talk to this superior and give him a piece of my mind. He can't blackmail you to do everything he wants you to."

"I agree, and after I run this errand for him I'll be sure to have a word. I need to put this man in his place. However, I know how these types work. I won't see him until after it's done. But you don't have the luxury of time, so no, you cannot join me. These projects often take weeks, if not months, to complete, depending on how bad the infestation is. Oftentimes the humans don't even know what they're looking at, much less *where* to look in terms of giving me an accurate idea of what's actually happening. If people are dying, this is far worse than they think. It's probably more than one creature, which is nothing I can't handle, but the last thing we need is Audrey going off the rails again."

"I can hear you," Audrey said from her place at the head of the table.

"The fact of the matter is, you have to go without me," Fyrn finished without acknowledging Audrey.

Victoria sighed. "We shouldn't go alone."

"You won't."

"But—"

Fyrn set his head in his hands. "I've arranged for Diesel to accompany you."

Victoria's mouth dropped open, and for a moment she couldn't speak. "You didn't."

Audrey burst into laughter, holding her sides as the realization hit her. "Oh my God, he totally *did*!"

Fyrn leaned back in his chair. "We don't have many options, Victoria. Diesel is the logical choice, even if you aren't very fond of him."

"*Not very fond of him?* I can't get a word in edgewise without him thinking I want him to autograph something!"

Audrey winked and pointed to her pants. "And by something, he means your—"

"Audrey! Not now!" Victoria could feel the heat in her face, but she couldn't tell if she was blushing or furious. Maybe a bit of both.

Fyrn leaned back in his chair. "Diesel is still a powerful wizard."

"But you're *more* powerful, and I actually like you."

"Really? I thought I was a grumpy old fart."

"I mean, you are, but you're still way better."

Fyrn chuckled. "You're not getting out of this, Victoria. Diesel is going with you. You need a guide who is experienced with magic. As much of a hassle as he is, Diesel is the second-best wizard in our city and one of the top hundred in the world."

Victoria couldn't suppress her smirk when Fyrn declared he was the best. Her mentor had confidence, even if he didn't have the public relations ability or charisma Diesel possessed.

She shook her head. "Please don't make me do this, Fyrn. There has to be another way."

"As I mentioned before there are always choices, but I don't like any of the ones we have here. Either Diesel goes with you or you wait until I return. I have no idea when that will be, so it doesn't make sense for that to be the choice. Besides, I'm making this one *for* you. You, Audrey, and Diesel leave first thing tomorrow morning. He's already been notified."

Victoria groaned loudly and slumped into the nearest chair, putting her hands on her cheeks she tried her best not to pout.

"Additionally, you must wear the diamond amulet," Fyrn said.

Audrey tilted her head, obviously confused. "Which—"

"The one my parents left in the vault?" Victoria asked.

Fyrn gestured toward Victoria's bedroom. "That one, yes. It will warn you of danger. I'm surprised you don't wear it at all times, with Luak after you."

Victoria shrugged. "It's a bit hard to train with it on. I'm not used to wearing jewelry."

"Get used to it. This necklace should never leave your body again. Understood?"

Victoria sighed. "I'll put it on before we leave."

Fyrn nodded. "Good. Now, Audrey... You need to pack every crystal you bought. Everything that has ever reacted to you is to go in a pouch that you keep on you at all times, for use in emergencies only. You must not touch any of them unless you absolutely have to. Do you understand?"

She pushed herself to her feet and nodded. "I'll be careful."

Fyrn pressed his fingertips together, staring at them as she left the room and headed upstairs. Several long seconds went by until they heard her bedroom door slammed shut and the floorboards creak in that section of the house.

"There's more, Victoria," he said softly.

"Then why did you wait for Audrey to leave?"

"She doesn't need to know what I'm about to tell you. I need you to promise that you'll keep this between us."

Victoria leaned back in her chair, studying him. "Why?"

"You'll see."

"I won't keep things from her."

"Even though she kept this magic from you?"

Victoria bit her tongue to prevent herself from saying something rash, and examined her hands.

Fyrn tapped his fingers on the table. "Victoria, Atlantis has its own artifacts. In fact, the Atlantean Artifacts are far more ancient than yours, and were the inspiration for the

Rhazdon Artifacts. They are quite similar, though the Atlantean Artifacts are gentler on the host. They possess only one power, rather than three, and they require much less sacrifice than the Rhazdon Artifacts do to fuse with them. I suggest you acquire some while you're in Atlantis. Buy them, steal them—I don't care. But you need to bring some home."

"You want me to steal? Who the hell *are* you?"

"I highly doubt they will sell them to you. You can try to buy one fair and square, but the Atlanteans are elitist, and they consider anyone who is not an Atlantean to be a mongrel or a servant at best. But Victoria, this could be what we've been looking for all along. The way for you to acquire the physical strength you need without taking on another Rhazdon Artifact. Isn't it worth a bit of theft to take out Luak? To keep him from killing anyone else?"

Victoria didn't even blink an eye. "I won't steal, Fyrn. It's wrong, and I'm disappointed you even brought it up."

Fyrn nodded. "As am I, to be honest, but I think you will change your mind when you meet them."

"They can't be that horrible."

Fyrn laughed, a deep and hearty laugh that shook his body. "Oh, you'll see."

"Look, if Audrey is Atlantean then they can't be that horrible. She's been with me through it all and has never once let me down."

Fyrn lowered his voice, his sharp eyes piercing Victoria. "Remember what Audrey is, child."

"She's my friend," Victoria said defiantly.

"Your friend, yes, but also an Atlantean. You must watch her. You must be careful. Atlanteans are inherently selfish, and you cannot rely on her to do anything that does not benefit her."

"It's like you don't know her at all," Victoria said, pushing herself to her feet.

"I do. I know her and I know you, but what you don't seem to understand is that the closer she gets to Atlantis, the harder it will be for her to remain the person you know. She will change, Victoria. The closer she gets to Atlantis, the louder the Atlantean within her will be and the harder it will be for her to resist it."

"But it's diluted, right? It's not like she's full-blooded Atlantean. She's human too, and by a large margin."

He nodded. "Atlantean magic is different, Victoria. It doesn't matter if there's the barest hint of Atlantean blood in her. The closer she gets to her homeland, the stronger it will become. She may not look like them, but they will know what she is almost instantly. They look out for their own, and no one else. When you get to Atlantis, you must look out for yourself, because you cannot rely on her to have your back."

Victoria shook her head. "You're wrong, Fyrn, and I can't wait to shove that in your face when we get back."

He sighed deeply and stood. "How often have I been wrong?"

Victoria suddenly found it very hard to breathe. His cold eyes pierced her and demanded she answer a question she wanted to leave hanging in the air. She met his gaze and refused to say a word, but deep down, she knew.

Fyrn didn't make mistakes. At least not anymore.

He seemed content to leave it at that and set a small vial of brilliant green liquid on the table, followed by a much larger container of the same potion. "Give her the small vial, but you keep the larger one. Don't tell her about the larger one, Victoria. It's your failsafe. Tell her to take this smaller potion while traveling to make sure that she doesn't destroy anything when she's in public. You're flying to Hawaii. Diesel has the map to take you from there, but we can't have her destroying the plane in midair. She needs to sleep for the entire flight. You understand?"

Victoria hesitated, taking the vial in her hand and studying the swirling liquid within. "She'll be okay? She will wake up?"

Fyrn nodded. "It's nothing more than a knockout potion to help her sleep and keep her from activating the lethal magic within her. You need to keep her sedated or at least groggy when she's in human places or she might expose the entire magical world. You know what would happen if she did that."

"She will be killed for treason."

He nodded. "If you want to protect her, you'll give her this for the plane."

Victoria almost handed it back, but his final words drove home her greatest fear. Right now Audrey needed to be protected from herself, at least until she mastered the powerful new magic within her. Victoria snatched the larger vial off the table and nodded. "Fine."

Her mentor headed to the front door. "Be safe, Victoria Brie."

"You too," she said as the front door shut.

Victoria looked at the stairs, ears craning to hear Audrey moving about her room. Floorboards creaked, and in the distance she heard the muffled thud of a drawer shutting. This was Audrey. This was her friend. They had promised to be together to the end, and Victoria wasn't going to be the one who broke that promise.

Even if Fyrn didn't believe in Audrey, Victoria always would.

CHAPTER THIRTEEN

"Hello, my love," a man said from the front hall.

Ugh. Victoria knew that voice. She had been playing with the diamond amulet around her neck, but cringed at the sound of his voice and braced herself for Diesel's arrogance. She didn't bother looking down the hallway toward the now-open front door. "Don't call me 'my love.' I don't even *like* you."

A few seconds later the pronounced thud of his boots on the hallway floor filled her foyer. His lofty frame and broad shoulders filled her doorway, and his black staff was as tall as he. The admittedly handsome young wizard smiled charmingly at her. He had sapphires sewn into the hem of his long white robes, and his long black hair streamed over his shoulders. A golden pendant hung from his neck nearly to his waist.

Diesel chuckled. "You know I love it when you play hard to get. It's obvious—you couldn't stay away from me, so you asked your mentor to arrange for me to guide you on a dangerous mission. It's actually sweet."

"That's not—"

"Victoria, have you seen that vial?" Audrey called from upstairs.

"On the counter in the kitchen." Victoria eyed the glowing bottle by the sink, and she tensed at Fyrn's warning about her friend. For a moment her worries let her forget about the smirking wizard in her kitchen.

Styx was rifling through one of the fruit baskets on the counter, preoccupied with devouring even more of her food. She leaned against the counter, fed up with the men in her life—even the tiny one.

"Ready for Hawaii?" Diesel asked, hands in his pockets. In any other circumstance she probably would have flirted with him for fun just because of his looks, if nothing else.

But this was *Diesel*. The first time they'd met, he had assumed she was a fan and had looked for something to autograph for her.

She sighed. Honestly, it wasn't fair that everything he said annoyed her. There was something about him that made her want to push him away, as though anything less than utter disdain would somehow be a failure on her part.

Maybe she should chill out. Be nicer. Let her guard down a bit. After all, he *was* helping them when they needed it most.

He pulled out a chair at the table and sat. "Hawaii would make a magnificent honeymoon spot, you know. We should go back after the wedding."

Nope, there was the asshole, right on cue.

"Will you drop the romance thing? I'm not interested."

"My, she doth protest too much!" He grinned. Any

other girl would have found his smile charming, but Victoria just wanted to hit something.

Preferably his face.

Instead of smacking him, Victoria unrolled the map on the kitchen counter. She hadn't had a chance to look at it yet, but she trusted Fyrn.

It was blank.

There were only two items on the parchment. One was the same symbol she had seen on the crystal in Drefus' study. The large ornate "A" on the map had been drawn in ink that shimmered and moved as she stared at it, the lines never standing still for more than a second. Aside from that, there was only the sketch of a lagoon, with palm trees dotted along the sandy beach and a sunset on the horizon.

"It's blank," she said, seething.

Diesel peeked at the map and grinned. "Quite the contrary, my dear."

She gestured at the almost empty parchment. "What, the symbol? Or the drawing of a beach? How is this going to get us to Atlantis?"

He settled deeper into his chair, that obnoxious but charming smile still on his face. "You'll see."

"Don't you do that. Don't you *dare* do that! I get enough of that from Fyrn, and I don't need it from you too."

That only made Diesel smiled wider.

She smacked her fist on the table. "Look, you—"

Booted feet thundered down the stairs and Audrey appeared in the hallway a few seconds later. Her eyes scanned the counters, finally settling on the glowing vial. "This is it, right?"

Victoria nodded and tossed it to her friend, who caught it easily.

Audrey examined it, holding it to the light as she hesitated. "I drink this now?"

"You don't have to."

"I don't want to blow up the plane, now do I?"

Diesel shuddered. "Hey, enough of that talk! Wizards hate flying enough as it is."

Victoria smirked, armed with a new weapon in their war. "Flying scares you?"

"Nothing scares me," he said with a defiant tilt to his chin.

"Except massive metal contraptions with stationary wings."

Diesel's smile faltered, but to his credit he recovered quickly. "Flying takes too long. I prefer more immediate gratification."

He winked.

Victoria groaned and rolled her eyes at the innuendo. She had a feeling that would happen a lot during their trip.

"Wait, how are we going to get onto a plane dressed like this?" Audrey glanced from her corset and white blouse to Victoria's knee-high boots and pinstripe leggings. Diesel stood out worst of all with that massive black wizard's staff and his robes.

Victoria paused, wondering. "True. We don't have our street clothes anymore."

"I'll cast a glamor," Diesel said.

"Glamor?"

"I'll use magic to change your appearance. Humans

won't see our clothes at all. I can even change our facial structures, if you'd like."

"Good idea," Victoria said, hating to admit he was right about something.

"Oh, not you, precious one. The world deserves to see your beauty."

"Thanks," Audrey said dryly.

Victoria groaned.

"Well, let's get this over with. Down the hatch," Audrey said, throwing back the green potion like a shot of tequila.

Diesel stood. "That takes thirty minutes to kick in. You'll be able to walk, but you won't feel or remember much. We'll take care of you."

He gestured toward the front door, and Audrey threw on her pack before heading out. Victoria sighed and brushed past the chair Diesel had left out from under the table, refusing on principle to push it in for him like a maid. Styx flitted out of the fruit basket and chased her, a few of the tangerines bouncing onto the floor from the force of his exit.

No map, a drugged best friend, and a guide who was like a younger, more annoying version of Fyrn.

This would be a long trip.

Fifteen hours later Victoria stood on the edge of a Hawaiian lagoon, lost in the beautiful vista. This small section of the Maui coastline had brilliant turquoise water and a sky dotted with thin wispy clouds. The sun beamed on her back, tanning her as the wind rattled the nearby palm trees. For several minutes the crash of waves on the beach sang her a welcome song.

"Pinch me," she said wistfully.

Beside her, she felt Diesel lean closer. It was an intuitive thing, one based on instinct rather than observation, and she swatted away his hand before it could reach her butt.

"Watch it," she snapped.

He chuckled.

"Pretty," Audrey said, blinking slowly as she stared out over the lagoon. She swayed, and Victoria grabbed her friend's arm to help keep the girl balanced. The potion had hit during check-in and lasted their entire flight, which had made security especially entertaining. Fyrn probably hadn't been on a flight in the last decade, so he hadn't realized how suspicious a stumbling girl who couldn't keep her arm raised in the body scanners might look. It had taken a bit of sweet-talking on Diesel's part—and a compliance spell or two—to get them through.

At least he was good for something.

Styx sunbathed on her shoulder, not bothering to move as she got her bearings. Victoria unfurled the Atlantean map, and Diesel snapped his fingers. A ripple of light surrounded them in an orb similar to Fyrn's bubble of silence back at the crime den, but this one stretched twenty feet in each direction.

"Won't people see us?" Victoria asked.

"Not at all, dearest. We're hidden. To any looking on, we simply disappeared into thin air. No one outside the circle will see anything that happens inside." He raised his brow suggestively.

She rolled her eyes. "Yeah, 'Stockholm Syndrome' me into a relationship. That's working great."

He chuckled. "Isn't that all flirting is?"

"Splish, splash," Audrey said, laughing as she jumped around in the water.

Jesus, this potion lasted forever, and instead of knocking her out she seemed more loopy than anything else. Keeping Audrey in line during the flight had been like trying to shepherd a drunk toddler. She had continuously thrown her complimentary pretzels at the flight attendant.

"Here," Diesel said, reaching for the map.

"No thanks," Victoria said. She stuck it under her arm while she pulled Audrey back onto the beach.

"I'm only trying to help." Diesel set a warm hand on Victoria's back, and his touch ignited a spark of something tingly in her core. She silenced it almost instantly and stepped out of his reach, but she couldn't speak for a second afterward. Maybe he had put a spell on her, or—

She cleared her throat, not sure what to say as she unfurled the map again. "I'm good, thanks."

The moving, shimmering symbol was now the only thing on the parchment. The image of the lagoon had disappeared. Victoria smacked it with the back of her hand. "See, Diesel? We're worse off than before."

"Face the water."

She frowned, but ultimately complied. She stood in front of the water and stared at the map, tapping her foot and annoyance.

As she watched, the symbol disappeared entirely and a single line of elegant text appeared in its place.

Ne intraveritis et susceperint vos domus.

Diesel stood behind her and leaned over her shoulder, his chin too close to her neck. "Enter and be welcomed, family."

"You speak Atlantean?" Victoria inched away to reclaim her personal space.

"It's Latin. And there's a lot you don't know about me, dearest." He winked.

Ugh.

Diesel pointed to the parchment. "Say those words."

Audrey hopped into the water again, giggling as she kicked and sent water high into the air. "Splashy!"

Victoria sighed. *"Ne intraveritis et susceperint vos domus."*

The ground rumbled underneath them, and waves crashed harder against the beach. The sand beneath Audrey began to crumble, and Victoria grabbed her arm just in time as a stairwell appeared beneath her. The wet-sand stairs descended into the ocean, which swept aside to allow them through as if the water were pushed up against an invisible barrier. At the bottom was an ornate set of double doors made from the sand itself. Seashells acted as handles, a warm and welcoming invitation inside.

So much for the theory that the Atlanteans were hostile people. The beautiful island, the gorgeous entry, the sweet saying... All of it seemed more welcoming than even Fairhaven. After all, during her first few weeks in Fairhaven she had been insulted by ogres and chased down thieves.

Hell, maybe she needed to move to Atlantis.

"Fuck! My head," Audrey said, hands on her temples. She slumped into the sand, elbows on her knees as she cradled herself.

Victoria knelt and rubbed her friend's back. "How are you feeling?"

"Terrible. What the hell was in that potion?"

"No idea, but it's Fyrn, so you probably drank toad mucus and cuss words. The good news is, you didn't kill us. We're here."

"Here." Diesel knelt on the other side of Audrey and set his hand on top of Victoria's. He muttered something under his breath, and warmth rushed through Victoria's hand into Audrey's body. Tingles of comfort radiated up Victoria's arm, a sensation that made her think about chicken soup and her mother reading to her when she was a kid.

Victoria snatched her hand away and stood, backing away from the wizard and whatever he was doing to help Audrey feel better. Startled, Styx darted into the air and hovered, a concerned expression on his tiny face. Audrey relaxed under Diesel's touch with a soft smile on her face, but Victoria couldn't stand the memories Diesel's spell had brought to the surface. For Victoria, what should have felt like comfort and joy just reminded her of what she didn't have any more.

A knot balled in her throat, and tears burned the corners of her eyes.

"Victoria?" Diesel stood, a look of concern on his face.

Victoria shoved her feelings down and shook her head. "I'm fine. Focus on Audrey."

She turned her back on the pair of them and stared down the steps to the door hidden deep in the ocean water. *She had to focus. She had to be present and aware.* This mission was about taking care of Audrey, not reliving her pain.

Diesel set a hand on her shoulder. It caught her off-guard, and she flinched. His touch was tender, which was more than she would have thought a cocky guy like him could muster. He hesitated, lips parted a bit as though he hadn't quite figured out what he had done wrong, and Victoria didn't correct him. The last thing she wanted to do was open up to Diesel, of all people.

"Audrey, are you okay?" she asked.

Audrey jumped to her feet and smiled. "That was the best hangover remedy I have ever had in my life. Thanks, Diesel."

"Anything for my favorite lady's best friend," he said, flashing that charming grin again.

Aaaaaand he's back.

"Let's go," Victoria said, jogging down the steps with Styx in tow. As she descended, fish swam in the lagoon on the other side of the barrier. Tinted light filtered into the stairwell through the waves above. Eventually she went through the lagoon's bottom into the sand below, Diesel and Audrey following closely. Victoria careful to keep the map as dry she could.

"Allow me." Diesel reached for the door handle.

She laughed. "I can open doors."

"Of course, but I would rather any attacks hit me instead of you."

"What attacks? Everything's been beautiful and welcoming so far."

"When in foreign territory, never allow yourself to become complacent." He gently tapped his staff against his head to drive the point home and opened the door carefully, sticking his head through before allowing it to open all the way.

Inside was a magnificent cave filled with light and white stone pathways. On either side of the path were pools of glittering clear water. Victoria couldn't tell where the light was coming from, but it was as bright down here as it had been on the island. It seemed to radiate from everywhere and nowhere, illuminating every nook and cranny with enough light to give the space an open and airy feel despite the rock walls around them.

A wide walkway covered in sand led the way through the mystical cave as though there weren't an ocean overtop. If anything, it seemed as though they were in whitewashed tunnels beneath a mountain, not a sea.

It was as though they had been transported into a completely different place, with shimmering green ferns growing from the very walls. Brilliant pink and purple flowers bloomed everywhere, hibiscus blossoms and others Victoria couldn't name. The walkway meandered through the caves before ending at a carved doorway that led to another tunnel.

The door slamming behind her finally snapped Victoria from her awestruck daze. As the sand doors closed, the rush of ocean water pummeling them sent her pulse skyrocketing with the fear that the water would break through. But the flood didn't come, and after a few seconds all was still and quiet once more.

"Wow," Victoria said under her breath. She returned her gaze to the dazzling cave, drinking in the scene before her as though she would never be allowed to see it again.

"Shall we?" Diesel gestured to the door on the far side of the cavern.

Still dazed, Victoria nodded gently and forced herself to lift the map. Before her eyes, the Latin words disappeared and a hand-drawn version of the scene before them appeared in their place. A blue arrow sketched on the ground led toward the tunnel.

"I guess we go that way."

"Well, what are we waiting for?" Audrey jogged ahead, a broad smile on her face, and Victoria couldn't help but smile back.

At least *someone* was enjoying herself.

A sense of nostalgia overwhelmed Audrey, growing stronger with every step she took into the tunnels beneath the lagoon that had welcomed them to the outskirts of Atlantis. She didn't know for sure these were the outskirts, but some silent impulse told her she was right. Walking through these caves was like Christmas morning or, better yet, it was like pulling into the beach town where her family had vacationed every single summer since she was three. The feeling warmed her like a campfire and produced a smile she could not have removed from her face even if she had wanted to.

Walking through these corridors was like coming home.

Every corner revealed a surprise. Every cave was filled with light and plants and flowers that made Audrey grin with delight. Each pool of water held vibrant fish in every color of the rainbow, reminding her of an aquarium at an expensive restaurant...except this was far better.

And with every step, the voice in the back of her head grew a little bit stronger. This was the voice that had told her to keep the white stone figurines a secret. The voice told her where to go, directing her through the labyrinth before Victoria even opened her map.

Audrey didn't say a thing as she walked forward. The voice spoke to her, and she ignored it. But with every step, it became louder. It became harder to disregard.

The impatient voice was pulling her toward something. Something spectacular. And the closer she got to it, the harder it became to tell the voice from her own thoughts.

CHAPTER FOURTEEN

"I sn't this magnificent?" Audrey lounged by one of the dozens of identical pools in the labyrinth of tunnels that led to Atlantis.

Victoria shrugged. "I mean, it's beautiful, don't get me wrong, but if it wasn't for the map we would be hopelessly lost. I'm glad we didn't try to get you here without it."

Audrey's smile faltered, but she didn't say anything. Her sense of direction was better down here than it had ever been anywhere else. She always seemed to know exactly where to go. Once again, however, that silent instinct not to share this new tidbit of information overpowered her impulse to tell Victoria everything.

It was true, though. Every tunnel and underground cave looked the same. They were all beautiful, covered in ferns and flowers that never got old, filled with pools of glittering clear water that could be mistaken for piles of diamonds at times.

The only difference was the wildlife. The deeper they

went into the network of caves, tunnels, and pools, the more creatures they discovered.

"Look!" Victoria pointed into one of the pools nearby. Aside from the fish that swarmed within, a large turtle swam close to the surface. A bump in the water appeared over its head, pushing through the rippling waves as it passed beneath their walkway. It emerged on the other side, its shell glittering with an iridescent sheen. As it passed, a frog peeked out from behind a leafy plant and hopped into the pool.

Audrey smiled. She never wanted to leave.

Diesel said something under his breath to Victoria, who rolled her eyes. Audrey chuckled. If Victoria rolled her eyes any more, they might fall out of her head.

Something deep in her chest pulled Audrey down the next tunnel. It wanted her to continue, even though her friends wanted to rest. She wasn't tired. She couldn't possibly be still, not with the beauty around her and the sense of nostalgia that drove her forward. Some distant part of her longed to be here, to get to their destination and never leave.

If only they would move faster!

The sudden pang of frustration was followed by a wave of guilt. She tried to shove the thought back into the recesses of her mind, tried to pretend that it hadn't popped up, but it had felt almost violent.

She wanted to get to Atlantis, and she wanted to get there *now*.

She stood, dusting off her pants and pretending to look into another of the pools while Victoria and Diesel bantered. She wondered if Victoria would ever cave and date the handsome wizard, and honestly, it was probably inevitable. The pretty guy always got the pretty girl.

A fizzle of jealousy burned in Audrey's chest, and she grimaced as she forced it back down.

"You guys ready to go?" she asked without turning around.

"Sure," Victoria said, a twinge of annoyance in her voice.

Audrey's first impulse was to spin around and tell her the attitude wasn't necessary. It took Audrey a moment to realize Victoria was probably annoyed at Diesel, not her.

Again she swallowed the resentment she didn't fully understand, and followed the voice in her core that told her where to go.

"You want to wait to know where we're going?" Victoria asked. Audrey knew her friend well enough to hear the smile on her face without even turning around.

Don't need you to tell me.

"Sure," Audrey said, waiting by the tunnel her intuition had pointed her toward.

Victoria lifted the map and pointed to the tunnel just past Audrey's head a few seconds later. "Lucky guess, *chica*."

"Must have been," Audrey said, with a hint of a smile.

Down here she didn't need luck. She just needed patience.

CHAPTER FIFTEEN

"You have five seconds to tell me where Victoria Brie is," Luak seethed.

He had pinned the massive ogre against the wall by her throat. For most Light Elves this would have been difficult, if not impossible, but Luak had immense power. He accessed the magic deep within one of his Rhazdon Artifacts to keep her immobile, allowing her to think it was his strength.

To her credit, the ogre didn't cower. Most in her position begged, doing anything it took for a few more seconds of life. She simply scowled at him, glaring as though she would kill him with a look.

Her five seconds passed, and she hadn't said a thing.

He laughed and dropped her. She hit the floor with a loud crash that rattled the nearby shelves. He was amazed the heavy ogre hadn't fallen through the floor and landed in the basement.

Her name was Bertha, if his memory served. He slowly paced the ogre's store, examining the various items and sampling a few of them. Succulent roast duck, a collection of the most delicious steamed vegetables he had ever eaten in his life, and an elegant four-tier chocolate cake were just a few of the dishes magically preserved on her shelves.

To be honest, this ogre was one of the few he *didn't* want to kill. As a longtime resident of Fairhaven, food was one of his few pleasures. It would have been a shame to waste talent such as hers.

Besides, he had a better idea.

"Stop toying with me and get on with it," the ogre said, not bothering to stand.

Luak watched her, letting the silence and the possibility of death weigh on her more heavily than a brandished knife or threat of violence ever could. Her hand trembled for the barest of seconds, and he figured if she had been standing her knees would've shaken.

She was a brave creature, but even brave creatures didn't want to die.

"But you *are* a toy, ogre, and I enjoy playing. It seems like you need time to think about my request, so you will live to see another day. In fact, you get to live until Victoria returns. If you want to live past then, you will tell me the moment she arrives."

He left without another word or glance back. He wasn't an idiot, and he knew Bertha wouldn't come to him. He knew loyalty when he saw it, and he found it to be a most annoying trait in his prey. He would likely have to kill Bertha eventually—much to the dismay of the culinary community—but examples had to be made. He would at least make it a painless death, unless she annoyed him further.

For now, Bertha was bait. Her home would be continuously monitored.

He passed an alleyway draped in shadows and, without stopping, nodded toward a creature lurking beside the brick wall. "Watch her."

"Yes, sir," the dark and gritty voice said.

Luak continued down the empty street, admiring his handiwork. The villagers were scared, and had been scarred by the disappearances of friends and family and strangers from the streets. No one came out unless they had to. Commerce had all but stopped, and the economy was choked.

The king had banished Luak, sure, but nothing had changed.

After Victoria had defeated his snarx and removed the king's fear, Luak had been forced to change his plans. Everything was still in the works, though. In fact, it was coming together faster than it would have before, so in a way he should have been grateful to the obnoxious brat for throwing a wrench into everything. He would still have Fairhaven, and he would still have Victoria. This time, though, he wouldn't let her slip out of his grasp. He would take her quietly out of the city and dispose of her in a landfill.

Provided he could find her, of course.

An itch burned along his spine as the ghost in his favorite Rhazdon Artifact, the one that gave him fire, expressed its displeasure with him. He didn't blame it. Luak himself was disgusted that he had let Victoria out of his sight, but he hadn't had a choice.

He had plans for Fairhaven, and they hinged on the

powers of her artifact. If he didn't get Victoria's artifact, he would fail. And if he failed, his master wouldn't be pleased. Very few survived her displeasure.

Anything less than success meant certain death for him. Luak would do everything in his power, kill anyone it took, and destroy everything in his path to get Fairhaven and turn it over to his master.

Right now, only one girl stood in his way.

CHAPTER SIXTEEN

Victoria sat in yet another of the caves, leaning against a wall and watching Audrey dip her fingers into the cool water. In all their time together, Victoria had never seen Audrey so happy. It was almost like watching someone discover beauty for the first time. Audrey danced her finger along the pool's surface, mesmerizing the fish beneath her. They swam after her, circling as each tried to nibble on her fingertip. She laughed, an enchanting smile on her face. Styx, meanwhile, buzzed the water, his tiny fingers grazing the surface as he flew.

The sound of footsteps on the sandy floor broke Victoria's reverie, and she looked up at the wizard as he sat down beside her. He nestled close to her, their shoulders touching despite there being plenty of wall to lean against, but she didn't bother sighing or rolling her eyes. It wouldn't have done any good, so she wasn't going to waste her energy complaining.

Besides, it had become chilly as they descended into the labyrinth, and he was warm.

He set his staff against the wall beside him and rested one elbow on his knee as he, too, watched Audrey play with the water. "She's like a different person down here."

"I hadn't noticed," Victoria lied. It was an impulsive lie, one she didn't fully understand. After she thought it over for a few seconds, she figured she had spoken so quickly because she didn't want to show her cards to Diesel. Her goal was to keep him at a distance emotionally. It would have been great if she could keep them at a distance physically, too, but that was a fight she wouldn't win. What he lacked in humility, he made up for in persistence.

He nudged her gently with the shoulder. "It's okay to be a little jealous."

Victoria didn't bother censoring herself. She shot him a glare full of annoyance and frustration. "I'm happy for her, not jealous."

"Are you sure?"

"Why on Earth would—"

"We're not *on* Earth, at least not the Earth you know. We're in Atlantis, her home country, where she will be welcomed like family. That incantation wasn't for us, Victoria. It was for her. We're not Atlantean. We are *not* their family. You may find that she likes it here better than back in Fairhaven."

Victoria shook her head. "You wizards. You fight and bicker, but you're all the same. You're full of ominous warnings and vague threats, but offer nothing of substance except your spells. Audrey is my friend, and she will *always* be my friend. She's discovering a part of herself she didn't know existed, magic she didn't know was there, and I'm going to support her every second of the way through it."

Diesel lifted his hands in gentle surrender and leaned his head against the wall as he stared straight ahead. "I didn't mean to offend you, Victoria. I merely want you to be prepared."

She didn't bother responding. It was uncanny how like Fyrn Diesel could be, and not in the fun ways. Fyrn challenged her, made her better. Diesel was just annoying.

They sat together in silence, watching Audrey as a large turtle swam up to her. It bumped its head against the palm of her hand as if begging to be petted, and she scratched its neck. It shivered in the water, and Victoria swore she could see a smile stretch across its face.

"Does this make me a Disney Princess?" Audrey asked with a wink and a smile.

Victoria nodded. "You'd better start singing."

Audrey chuckled and continued to pet the massive turtle. This was unreal. Next thing they knew, birds would fly out of the holes in the cave wall and nestle in Audrey's hair.

A blip of golden light in the corner of her eye caught Victoria's attention. She turned in time to see the light recede into Diesel's hand, where he now held a stunning golden dagger. It had been crafted of a single material from blade to handle, and the metal glistened and churned like water against a transparent surface.

He offered it to her. "Consider this an olive branch, Victoria. I want you to have it."

Victoria didn't know what to say. She lifted it with her fingertips, and it was surprisingly light. She grasped it in one hand, and the hilt fit perfectly into her palm. "It's beautiful."

"It's powerful, too."

"How so?"

"If you stab someone with it, they are forced to speak the truth."

She scoffed. "Are you sure that's not from the pain of being stabbed?"

He chuckled and shook his head. "This won't make you bleed. It's special."

The delicate weapon felt like air in her palms. "So it's a 'truth dagger,' huh?"

"I figured you weren't the kind of girl who would care about a dozen roses, so I'm giving you a truth dagger instead."

She shook her head at his obnoxious persistence, but she couldn't hide her smile. "How does it work?"

"Stab me."

She quirked an eyebrow. "You're not *that* annoying."

He winked. "Not yet, anyway. Go ahead. Anywhere."

Doubtful, she hesitated. "I don't want to hurt you."

"It won't hurt at all. Think of a question you want to ask me and stab my leg. Anything goes."

"Suit yourself." She pressed the tip of the blade against his thigh, but he didn't flinch. She pressed gently on the hilt, and it slid effortlessly into his body without drawing a single drop of blood. The blade simply disappeared into the fabric covering his leg.

Instead of screaming with pain, he shuddered. "Brr. I forgot how cold it is. Ask me something."

"Why did you come with us?"

He caught her eye, jaw tense and lips parted slightly as though he were fighting the words about to tumble out of his mouth. "I wanted to make sure you were safe. Few return from Atlantis, and no one is the same when they come back. I knew you would try to go alone, and I wanted to protect you from getting hurt."

She quirked an eyebrow. "I'm pretty sure that would have been your answer even if I hadn't stabbed you with a truth sword."

"Dagger."

"Whatever."

"Out, out, pull it out," he said, body tensing.

She obliged him and studied the dagger, still not convinced.

"I can try it on you," he said.

She studied him for a moment, wondering if this were a trick. Diesel was her mentor's foe, after all, and one she barely trusted. If this really was a magic dagger, he could pry any information he wanted out of her.

"Only if you want," he said softly, looking away.

His deference caught her off-guard. He was usually so cocky, so sure of himself, that his quiet offer surprised her. Taken aback, she hesitated. It almost seemed like the deeper she got into these caves, the less she knew the people she was with.

"Fine," she said, offering the blade.

He took it. "What shall I ask?"

"Nothing too personal."

"Very well." He paused to think for a moment before setting the tip of the blade against her thigh. "Are you ready?"

She nodded, tensing as she prepared for pain. He gently slid the dagger into her leg, and instead of agony she felt only the cool chill of frost on her skin. It was like stepping outside in winter with no jacket. She shivered. "Oh, Jesus, that *is* cold."

He nodded. "What do you think about Fairhaven?"

Words pressed against her tongue like a mob against a locked gate. She tensed, already hating the feeling of these words desperate to tumble out of her. Her mouth finally opened on its own, and she had no idea what she would say. "I love Fairhaven. It's my home."

Diesel smiled, the creases around his eyes suggesting genuine happiness. "I'm glad to hear that."

She reached for the dagger to pull it out, but it was as though there were a forcefield preventing her from touching the hilt while it was in her leg. She waved at it, panicking a bit. "Out, out, out."

"Sorry, yes." He pulled it out of her leg and warmth returned to Victoria's body in a rush. She sighed with relief and shut her eyes, slumping against the wall with gratitude that the thing was out of her.

In her haste to get the dagger out of her body she had let her sleeve slide up her arm and reveal the Rhazdon Artifact embedded in her skin. Diesel's eyes wandered over it, studying its curves and grooves, and for a moment Victoria let him. She watched his face, examining every expression, and was surprised to see only curiosity and calm. His eyes eventually met hers, and she waited for him to say something.

"It's fascinating," he said.

"What is?"

He nodded to her arm. "From everything I have learned, from every book I have read and every master I have spoken to, you should be utterly and completely evil. You should want nothing more than to rip the skin from my body and steal whatever magic you can. You should be an insatiable monster, content with nothing less than domination and power. And yet... "

She waited, tense and uneasy as she watched him search for the words he wanted.

He continued, "And yet you're not. You're beautiful and kind and powerful and loyal. You're the kind of person I would follow into battle without a second thought."

He stood and returned to their packs, which they had left a few feet from the walkway while they rested. He rummaged through his, but Victoria suspected he was merely occupying himself. She was suddenly convinced that even if she hadn't used the dagger, he would have told the truth anyway.

Elbow on her knee, she stared at the sandy floor as she tried to process what he had said. If she were being honest with herself, it was nice to be appreciated and not feared.

Her eyes wandered to Audrey, who was already staring at her. Neither said anything. Audrey eventually returned her attention to the pool of water, but her smile was gone.

———

Victoria had stopped trying to keep track of the hours they spent in the caves beneath Hawaii looking for Atlantis. They halted when they were tired, ate when they were hungry, and continued to follow the map.

But the more they walked, the more Victoria realized Audrey seem to know where she was going without referencing the scroll. Sometimes Victoria would wait until Audrey had already begun walking before checking the map. Audrey had been right every time. It bothered Victoria more than she felt it should, leaving her uneasy.

Hell, maybe she had wasted that favor to a crime boss to get this map. The thought alone annoyed her.

Around another bend, a fork in the tunnel forced Victoria to refer the map. But instead of another sketch directing her where to go, more words appeared on the parchment.

Progredere iudicari.

"Okay, no clue how to say that one," Victoria muttered.

Diesel peered over her shoulder, too close again. "I wasn't expecting that."

"What? What does it say?"

"Step forward and be judged," Audrey said in an airy voice, as though she were deep in thought.

"Exactly," Diesel said warily, eyes shifting toward Audrey.

Victoria jerked her head toward her friend, baffled and confused. "How did you know? You didn't even look at the map."

Audrey didn't answer. She stared into one of the tunnels, head cocked as though she were listening for something that Victoria couldn't hear. "They're coming."

"Who?"

Audrey turned around, and for a moment Victoria didn't recognize her. Audrey's eyes were unfocused, and a strange smile played on her lips. It was as though someone had possessed her, and for a moment Victoria was terrified.

Physical attackers she could handle, but not a possessed bestie.

Her diamond amulet began to glow.

Danger.

Diesel put his hand on Victoria's shoulder, and for the first time she wasn't annoyed. She appreciated the comfort it brought, and it took a moment to realize she had leaned toward Audrey and the hand was holding her back.

"Don't," he said quietly.

"Who dares enter the secret lands?" A man's voice echoed through the tunnel, as warped and distorted as if he were talking underwater.

Styx squeaked in surprise and dove into Victoria's hair, his tiny body trembling.

The thundering voice seemed to snap Audrey out of her daze. She came to, looking around with wide eyes. But instead of fear, she looked excited—as if she were ready and waiting for something Victoria couldn't see.

Victoria would have given anything to know what was going on in her friend's head.

There was a sudden presence behind Victoria, the kind of feeling that came when someone walked into a room. She spun on her heel to find a man behind her. His silver skin looked as soft as silk, and it had a slight iridescent gleam that reminded Victoria of wet scales. His long black hair hung over his shoulders, and he held a curved sword in each hand. He glowered at Victoria, his eyes shifting between her and Diesel.

Victoria tensed, ready to summon her sword, but Diesel caught her eye and shook his head gently. It was a warning, a request for her to stand down, so she hesitated.

She shot a wary glance around. Light glinted from dozens more swords in the shadows of both tunnels behind Audrey. The way toward Atlantis was blocked, and this solitary stranger stood between them and the way out.

But leaving wasn't the goal—they needed to reach Atlantis. Victoria tensed and waited for something to happen.

The stranger looked past them both, his eyes scanning something Victoria could only assume was Audrey. His scowl was immediately replaced by a broad grin, and he pushed past Victoria as though she weren't there. Victoria stumbled into the wall, and Diesel reached for her to help her find her feet again.

"I'm fine," she said, waving away his hand. The stranger walked up to Audrey, who studied him with concern.

He offered his hand to her, and she nervously took it. When she touched him he muttered something under his breath, and as if on cue her skin began to glow a brilliant blue. She rose into the air and hovered, her hair floating around her head as though she were swimming underwater, the ribbons of her dark locks shimmering like silk. But instead of showing fear or concern, she smiled down at the stranger.

"What a happy day!" the stranger said. He clasped her wrists and guided her to the ground as the soldiers in both tunnels began to cheer. The sound reverberated off the walls, shaking Victoria to her core.

"Am I really Atlantean?" Audrey asked, almost breathless.

"Quite so, young one. Quite so. I am General Cato, dear soul. And you are?"

"Audrey."

"An honor to meet you, Miss Audrey. Come, come! We must bring you home at once!"

The cheering continued as the general led Audrey down one of the tunnels, and the soldiers parted to let them through. But instead of waiting for Victoria and Diesel to catch up, the soldiers closed the path again and began to follow their general as though neither Victoria nor Diesel were even there.

"Hey!" Victoria shouted.

Diesel grabbed her arm. "Victoria, remember the Atlantean way. We don't exist to them. They care only for their fellow Atlanteans."

"But who knows if she's safe with them? I just let my friend disappear into a crowd of strange men. Do you know how wrong that would be?" Victoria jogged after them, and Diesel kept pace with her.

"Trust me, Victoria, *she's* safer with them than you or I are." He shot her a glance that made Victoria feel like he knew more than he was letting on.

It finally struck her as they jogged after the soldiers, who were still cheering for her friend. Diesel had come to protect Victoria, not because he was enamored of her, but because Audrey was not in any kind of danger. These were Audrey's people, and it was suddenly very clear that Victoria was not welcome.

CHAPTER SEVENTEEN

A*tlantis is beautiful.* It was all Audrey could think as she took in the magnificent hidden city around her. A long transparent bridge allowed her to walk over a dazzling lake, and it ended at a massive palace with spires and glittering blue floor-to-ceiling windows covering the entire edifice. On either side of the walkway, the world stretched for what seemed like miles in an impossibly massive underground cavern that didn't have a hint of darkness. It glimmered and gleamed, glowing with its own light even though she couldn't tell where it came from. The water sparkled like something in a commercial, too perfect to be real, and yet she was looking at it.

General Cato led her across the bridge, his hand on the small of her back the entire way. Ordinarily she would've batted him away, being perfectly able to walk by herself, but something about these people—something about their kindness and excitement at seeing her—melted her defenses. She lost herself in their joy.

Other Atlanteans strolling along the lakeside streets of

sand and cobblestone paused to watch the procession as it followed the glass road. Some waved, and others smiled happily at her.

She was welcomed here. Celebrated. The tiny internal voice she had been ignoring began speaking again, telling her this was where she belonged.

Audrey was so wrapped up in her surroundings that it seemed like they reached the castle in no time at all.

She almost couldn't believe her eyes when palace guards opened the vast double doors to the Atlantean palace for her. General Cato led the way, his hand still on the small of her back, and directed her toward the thrones at the back of the grand room. Their shoes tapped against the blue marble floor, but instead of observing the room, Audrey was instead captivated by the silver thrones and the beautiful Atlanteans sitting in them. Their soft skin shimmered in blues and greens. The man's long black hair fell down his back, and a brilliant silver crown sat atop his head. The woman beside him had long black hair woven into a delicate braid that dropped clear to her waist, and her silver crown bore glittering blue jewels on each of its points. Both smiled broadly as she approached them, and stood to greet her when the general knelt before them.

"Introducing Miss Audrey," General Cato said.

"We haven't met a new Atlantean in centuries," the king said.

The queen nodded. "It is an honor to meet you, young lady. Welcome to our city."

Audrey beamed. "This feels like a dream. Everything is so beautiful. I didn't think people could be this friendly."

The Atlantean woman laughed, the delicate sound

lighthearted and airy. "You're family, dear one. In Atlantis, we take care of our own. Come with me, Miss Audrey. I'm sure you'll want to rest after your travels, and we have prepared our finest guest room for you."

The queen began to lead Audrey from the throne room, but when she looked over her shoulder she realized Victoria and Diesel were gone. "Wait, where are—"

"Your servants will be fed and given their own quarters," the queen assured her.

Audrey laughed. She couldn't help it. The thought of anyone mistaking Victoria for her servant was too much. "They're not my servants."

Confused, the queen stared for a moment, then quickly glanced at the king and general as if they could explain the situation. Apparently neither knew what to say, and General Cato eventually gave a small bow. "Forgive us, dear Audrey, but what else could they be?"

"Guards!" the king said with a laugh. "They're her guards, of course."

Audrey chuckled, still entertained by their confusion. "They're my fr—"

"Forgive us," the queen interrupted with a laugh. "We were so excited to have you here, we weren't thinking. Your guards are safe. Come, I'll show you to your room."

When the queen began to lead her through the hall again, Audrey just shook her head and followed. They might have had some odd customs and made strange assumptions, but so far they had been nothing but polite. Audrey wasn't going to fight them. She could always correct them later.

The brilliant castle walls were as white as the sandy

beaches that had led them into the depths of the first caves on the way to Atlantis. Every window she passed offered a spectacular view of distant mansions or glimmering pools of water far below. There were brilliant green farms in the distance, and even a small forest. This cavern was its own ecosystem, full of life and vibrant color.

Eventually the queen pushed open a set of double doors that led to a beautiful and massive bedroom. In the center was a raised platform, and on the platform stood an ornate four-poster bed that looked out onto a balcony. A gentle warm breeze wafted past the curtains that hid the open balcony doors. It was perfect here, neither too hot nor too cold.

"Wow, that was fast," Audrey said.

The queen smiled. "Our servants were notified as you walked over the grand lake. We strive for perfection in all things, Miss Audrey, and no guest should ever be forced to wait to relax after a long journey."

"This is incredible," Audrey said with an admiring grin on her face.

On the bed lay a silky white dress and several towels. The queen gestured to the door on the far wall. "You have a full bathing room at your disposal, and several maids will provide whatever you need. Once you have freshened up, have one of them send for us. We've planned a small feast in your honor."

"Thank you so much," Audrey said with a warm smile.

The queen nodded and returned to the hallway, leaving the doors open as she left. Audrey now had views from two sides of the castle, and they were spectacular—nothing but clear water and beautiful homes. Now and again she would catch a glimpse of a dark-haired beauty strolling along one of the sandy walkways, a long dress trailing in her wake. It was so calm here, so joyful.

What had begun as a small voice in Audrey's head when she first touched the crystal in the marketplace had now became an overwhelming force that drove her thoughts. Atlantis was like nothing she had ever experienced in her life. This felt like heaven. Like happiness. Like *home*.

Victoria gaped at the empty room into which she and Diesel had been shoved by the guards who had led them through the castle. She still hadn't seen Audrey, and part of her worried for her friend. But based on the reception her friend had been given, Victoria figured it was more prudent for her to worry about herself at the moment.

The room she was supposed to share with Diesel contained nothing but a pile of hay and a loaf of brown bread on a plate on the floor. Along the far wall was a single window, barely wide enough for a head to fit through.

Diesel leaned in. "At least they gave us a plate. How generous."

Behind them, the door slammed. Both she and Diesel flinched and spun on their heels, but the door didn't have a handle from this side, and it opened inward.

"This is insane," Victoria said under her breath.

Diesel shrugged. "It's about what I was expecting. I had hoped I would be wrong."

"Do they hate everyone who isn't Atlantean?"

"Pretty much."

"They didn't even give us a bed! It's just hay!"

Diesel grinned. "A bed? You only want *one*?"

She shot him a pointed look. "Focus, Romeo. This isn't a room, it's a stall."

Diesel leaned against the wall and put his hands in his pockets. "Like I said, they only take care of their own."

Victoria placed her hands against the door, biting her tongue and shaking her head in an effort to keep from doing or saying something stupid. They had welcomed Audrey like royalty, but were treating Victoria and Diesel like cattle.

Styx fluttered overhead, his tiny wings beating the air with a slight hum that reverberated in the otherwise empty room. She beckoned him over.

"Go look for a vault or something like one. Let me know when you find it."

Still hovering in the air, Styx gave a salute before flittering off through the tiny window in the far wall.

"A vault, huh?" Diesel asked.

She met his gaze and dared him to challenge her, but he didn't. Instead, he pushed himself off the wall and begin to pace around the room, observing every brick as though it were interesting. Maybe he was looking for a secret passage or some other way out, but Victoria was too pissed to even think about escape.

She had sworn she wouldn't steal from the Atlanteans when Fyrn had suggested it, and he told her she would change her mind. She wasn't quite ready to steal anything, but she was sure as hell considering it.

These people were assholes.

CHAPTER EIGHTEEN

Later that evening, Audrey left her room in a magnificent white dress with a train that whispered over the floor as she walked. The soft fabric was unlike anything she'd ever felt and it fit her like a glove, flattering the curves she had always hidden beneath her jeans and baggy T-shirts. It was as though a permanent smile had been etched into her face, and her cheeks almost hurt from it.

She was off to a private dinner with royalty who wanted nothing more than to get to know her and ask her questions about her life.

A flare of warning crept into the back of her mind, a rare moment of sanity in the midst of the fanfare.

Ask yourself why, her intuition said.

This was different than the voice that had guided her through the labyrinth on the way to Atlantis. This was deeper and stronger—her real self, the natural intuition she had trusted since birth.

She paused in the center of the hallway, joy rushing

from her like water from a balloon. Since she had come here, she had listened only to the voice that had first appeared back in Fairhaven. The one that had told her to keep her magic a secret. That plan had failed and yet, the closer she got to Atlantis, the more she felt compelled to listen to that voice.

It was almost as though she wasn't in control of herself. And since she had been here, she had ignored her common sense almost completely.

She pressed herself against the wall and held her head as she tried to sift through her conflicting thoughts. She felt crazy, and legitimately wondered if she were losing her mind.

Atlantis did things to her, shifted her thoughts in a way she wasn't sure she liked. Moments of sanity weren't supposed to be few and far between—especially not for her.

Throughout her friendship with Victoria, V had been the bubbly fun one and Audrey had been the asshole who had kept people from taking advantage of her friend. Yet here Audrey was, without a clue as to where Victoria had even gone.

"Audrey?"

Audrey snapped upright. General Cato was standing at the end of the hallway and watching her with a concerned expression. In a matter of seconds he crossed the gap between them with his long, powerful strides.

"Are you all right?" He set a hand on her shoulder, and as quickly as her moment of sanity had come, a warm numbness took its place. Her worry faded with his touch, and the blissful happiness she had felt since entering the palace returned.

She still knew she was supposed to be worried about something, but she couldn't remember what.

"I'm fine," she said softly, not quite believing herself.

He smiled. "You must be hungry. I bet you haven't had real food in quite a while. Come with me. The king and queen are waiting for you in their private dining area. The royal family has taken quite a liking to you, you know. I have a feeling you will be joining them here frequently."

She grinned. "What a kind thing to say. Thank you. Do they have children?"

"Sadly, no. They've tried, but all their children died young. I think you remind them of—" The general cleared his throat and cast his gaze to the floor.

"Of whom?"

"I'm sorry, I shouldn't say. Perhaps the king will tell you someday, but it's not my place."

Deep in her chest, a warning flared like a bonfire through her body. Something was wrong about what he had just said, but she couldn't place it.

General Cato leaned in. "You'll have to act surprised when they share this with you, but I happen to know for a fact they'll be offering you training."

"Training?"

"Of course! You were raised by humans, so you have no idea what it means to be an Atlantean. We possess powerful magic, Audrey, and you need to learn to control it."

"That's actually why I'm here," Audrey said.

He tilted his head. "What do you mean?"

"I took out half a city block in Fairhaven when I lost control. I need to learn to manage this magic, or I might hurt somebody."

General Cato's smile widened, and he looked at her in appreciation. "I'm impressed, Audrey. Most Atlanteans don't realize their potential even when raised here. I expect great things from you, and I know you won't let me down."

"How could I? I feel at home here."

"You *are* home, Audrey."

She nodded without thinking, and the suspicious little voice in her core grew quiet again.

With every step Victoria took in the Atlantean palace, she became more and more uneasy.

A short while after they had arrived, the door had clicked open and a maid delivered a curt *"follow me"* before darting off. She and Diesel had obeyed simply to get out of the room, but the maid walked too quickly and they could barely keep up.

Out of spite, Victoria refused to walk any faster than a casual stroll, even if it meant getting lost.

Each soldier she passed glared at her as she walked by. Even the maids stared at her with a mixture of wariness and disgust. She hated it here. It felt as though they would kill her at any moment simply for not being Atlantean.

"Don't let them see that it gets to you," Diesel said softly from beside her.

Victoria tried to take his advice, arching her back and relaxing her shoulders as best she could, doing her best to keep her eyes forward. Diesel put his arm around her waist and nodded charmingly to the next maid they passed, who averted her eyes quickly and hurried down another hallway.

Victoria smacked away his hand and he chuckled. "I had to try."

"Focus, Diesel," she said under her breath.

"Do you know where we're going?" he asked, apparently trying to change the subject.

She shook her head. "I haven't seen that damned maid in at least five minutes."

"Where are you two going?" a man asked from behind them.

Victoria spun on her heel to find a guard in the middle the hallway, his shoulders squared and hand on his sword as he stared them down.

"We're looking for Audrey," Victoria said.

"She's with the king and queen, and you're not to interrupt. Go to her quarters, and she will give you instructions when she returns."

Victoria gaped when the guard summoned one of the maids from a nearby room and spoke to her in a language Victoria didn't understand. Diesel, to his credit, simply burst out laughing.

They thought she and Diesel were servants.

Without making eye contact, the maid gestured and began to head down a side hall. "This way."

Victoria could feel the heat in her cheeks, but did her best to restrain her boiling anger.

Unbelievable.

CHAPTER NINETEEN

Not long after her meal with the king and queen, Audrey had been ushered to one of the many palace gardens to begin her training. The ornate wrought-iron fences were covered in ivy and roses, and giant hedges surrounded her on all sides. To her left an Atlantean woman adjusted one of the dozens of glistening artifacts on display, almost all of them crafted from the same stone as those Audrey had bought in the Fairhaven marketplace. Most of them had been carved into beautiful animals, though some were unfinished crystal points.

The Atlantean instructor pulled her long braid over her shoulder and smiled warmly. "Do you know why some of them are carved into statues while others aren't?"

Audrey shook her head. "They're beautiful, though."

The instructor nodded. "Indeed they are. The weaker crystals are carved into statues or figurines while those with the most power are left untouched, preserving as much of the original stone and its power as possible. The weaker stones are made beautiful in a different way."

Audrey grinned, thinking of the stones hidden in her pack in her room. No wonder that one had given her so much power back in Fairhaven.

"As our honored guest, you may choose any of these you like. Which draws you?"

Audrey stood in front of the table, eyes wandering over the brilliant facets and edges of all the crystals. But one in the center caught her eye, a brilliant blue crystal about the size of a golf ball. She lifted it, and white light danced along her skin at its touch.

The instructor beamed. "You have a gift, Audrey. In all my years of teaching, only royalty has ever picked the most powerful stone the first time they tried."

Audrey smiled, pleased with herself.

"Let us practice your aim," the instructor said, gesturing toward a circular target at the end of the red brick path. Behind it was a tangle of vines and ivy dotted with pink flowers.

"How do I do this?" Audrey asked.

"Atlantean magic is all about intention and focus. The power is in your connection to the crystal you hold in your hand. Therefore, you need never question your ability, only where to channel the energy. There is limitless power in that crystal. However, as you are new to its magic, it will drain some of your energy as well with each shot. The more powerful your attack, the more of your own energy you will use—at least in the beginning. Over time, you will learn to overcome this fatigue, but don't be surprised if you find yourself winded in the early years of your training. Now, focus your mind and trust the power within the crystal you hold. Where would you like its magic to go?"

Audrey stilled, narrowing her eyes as she focused her attention on the target at the end of the path. There were three concentric circles, as was the case with most targets, and she focused on the centermost one.

"There," she said, pointing to it.

As if on command, a bolt of white light shot from her fingertip and struck the center of the target. Smoke billowed from the mark, and the fabric sizzled.

The instructor gaped at the burn in the center of the target. "Miss Audrey, forgive me if I've related basic things you already understood. I was under the impression you were new to Atlantean magic."

"Oh, I am. I don't have any control over this yet. That must've been luck."

The instructor shook her head. "No, my dear, that was skill. We will need to work on refinement and what to do if you're caught off-guard, but I'm astonished that we can proceed to such advanced conversations on the first day."

Audrey beamed with pride. Finally she was getting the hang of this magic of hers.

"The king and queen will be most pleased to hear this," the instructor said with a wink.

"I'm just grateful for the opportunity to train here," Audrey said.

"Keep impressing us, dear one, and you will get far more than training. Come, let us continue."

Audrey squared her shoulders, anticipation dancing along her fingers. She ached to access her magic once more.

This was too good to be true.

Audrey had lost track of how much time she spent in the palace gardens with the instructor, but they had covered immense ground in their training today. She had been thrown into uncomfortable situations where the magic had pushed against her skin, begging to be set free just as it had when she fought the monster in Fairhaven. This time she was able to keep her cool, and it paid off. She only lost herself to the magic once, and even then she had regained her composure quickly.

It wouldn't be long before she mastered this new magic well enough to return to Fairhaven.

She had returned to the hall where her room was located while she pondered her new situation. At the thought of leaving Atlantis, she hesitated. Her heart ached at the prospect.

Perhaps she should stay.

As she leaned against her bedroom door, something glimmered on her skin. She examined the back of her hand and found it had a slight sheen, not unlike the blue and green iridescence she had observed on all the Atlanteans here.

She smiled, her heart warming at the thought of fully embracing her Atlantean heritage. She had known things would change when she arrived in Atlantis, but she hadn't thought the changes would be literal. Her body was already adjusting to life in Atlantis.

"There you are," Victoria said from down the hallway.

Audrey looked up and saw Victoria carrying a handful

of towels and wearing a scowl that would wilt a flower. "What's wrong with you?"

Victoria let loose a humorless laugh. "What's wrong with me? Oh, I don't know—maybe the fact they think I'm your servant? I wasn't allowed up here without towels and a change of clothes for you."

Audrey couldn't help herself. She laughed. "Well now, servant girl, I don't see a dress."

Victoria shook her head, but even the towels couldn't hide her smile. "Fuck you."

Audrey chuckled and pushed the door open, holding it for her friend. "I've spent the last I-don't-even-know-how-many hours training. I've already got a bit of this magic stuff down, Victoria."

Victoria tossed the towels on the bed and laid back on the comforter, staring at the ceiling. "Thank goodness. Hopefully we won't have to stay very long."

Audrey's smile faded, and an irrational wave of anger crashed through her. She set her blue crystal on the bedside table and crossed her arms. "Why *wouldn't* we stay here? It's beautiful."

"Yeah, *your* room is. I'm in a stall with Diesel, sharing a bundle of hay."

Audrey rolled her eyes. "Stop exaggerating."

"I'm not. That's the pathetic part."

Audrey set her hands on her hips, disgusted that Victoria would be so disrespectful to the people who had been nothing but welcoming. "Look, okay, they mistook you for servants. I'm sorry, and I'll get it fixed. But come on, there's no need to be an ass. You're not literally sleeping in hay."

Victoria's rested on her elbows, narrowing her eyes a bit as she studied Audrey's face. "I'm a little worried about you."

"About me? Why?"

"I'm concerned you're getting caught up in the beauty of Atlantis, while ignoring the darker side of it. These people aren't as nice as they seem."

Audrey threw up her hands and began to pace around the room. "They don't fawn over you, you mean."

"Why would I want—"

"They have been completely delightful to me, Victoria, and maybe you don't like them because they aren't fawning over you like the people back in Fairhaven."

"Simmer down, Sally," Victoria said, rising to her feet. She leaned back, nose crinkled a bit as she gave Audrey a familiar look.

Audrey knew that expression. It said, "What's wrong with you?"

"Nothing's wrong with me," Audrey snapped. "It's you. Your attitude. You're trying to take away my heritage, the thing that makes me special, and I don't appreciate it. I don't want to leave yet, so don't rush me."

To her credit Victoria didn't say anything, but her expression shifted nonetheless. The look that followed was one Audrey had only seen a handful of times in her life, but she knew it all the same. It meant Victoria was biding her time, doing her best to figure out a different way to phrase what she wanted to say.

"Apologies, Your Highness," Victoria said snidely. She retreated from the room and slammed the door behind her.

The moment the door closed, a pang of guilt hit Audrey square in the chest. She leaned against the wall, another moment of sanity burning away the joy.

Had Fyrn's warning been correct? Was she losing herself to her Atlantean predisposition for selfishness?

Confused and not entirely sure if she could trust herself, Audrey slid down the wall until her butt hit the floor. She didn't want to lose Victoria, but she finally felt at peace. She finally felt like there was a gift within her as glorious and powerful as Victoria's.

Maybe even more so.

After so many weeks and months of living in strange places and being surrounded by strange creatures with customs Audrey didn't understand, she felt at home.

And not even Victoria will take that from me!

Audrey gasped, her hand on her mouth as she tried to suppress the nasty thought that had just arisen. She knew it hadn't been her. It had been foreign and desperate. In her core, she knew it had been that strange voice she had heard off and on since she found the crystals in the marketplace. With every hour she was here, it grew louder.

Victoria was right. Audrey needed to leave, to get out of here, to...

The glimmer of the blue crystal on her bedside table caught her eye, and she reached for it almost in a daze. The crystal settled into her palm, and her panic faded to a happy numbness. As it had in the hall when the general touched her, her worry abated. She still felt like she should be concerned with something, but she couldn't remember what.

"So strange," she murmured softly to herself.

CHAPTER TWENTY

Victoria paced the *stall* she shared with Diesel while she waited for him to return. They had to do something—*anything!*—to get Audrey back.

A few moments later the door creaked open and Diesel came in. Victoria couldn't stop pacing, however. She could barely think, much less form words. She was fuming.

"Victoria, darling—"

"Don't you 'darling' me."

A thin smile played at the corners of Diesel's mouth. "My love, please calm down. Whatever's bothering you, I'm sure we can find a solution."

"It's Audrey. She's not herself. She's in danger."

"Victoria."

"Whatever these people are doing to her is changing her entire personality—"

"Victoria, *please.*"

"—and I'm not going to sit idly by while—"

A chill swept through Victoria's body. Frost coated her skin, and she shivered. Diesel stepped up behind her, one hand on her shoulder as he pressed the truth dagger deeper. He must have grabbed it from her pack when she wasn't looking.

"Diesel, what on Earth—"

"What's the most disgusting thing you've ever eaten?" he asked.

For a moment she simply stared at him. It wasn't willpower that kept her answer at bay. It was shock. "That's the dumbest question I've ever heard."

"Exactly. Before we can get anywhere or make any plans, you need to relax. Now answer me."

The words pressed against her mouth as the dagger's magic swirled within her until she couldn't hold them back anymore. "My Mom's raspberry hot sauce omelet with broccoli and peppers. She loved that nasty heap of mismatched food."

"Oh gods, that's disgusting." Diesel grimaced, his grip loosening on the dagger.

"It really was. God, she would try to make me eat it all. If I smelled that cooking I snuck out the back door, even if I was starving." Victoria laughed at the memory of her mother insisting it wasn't all that bad. *Really* laughed. Her eyes watered and her cheeks hurt from the sheer improbability of a wizard stabbing her with a truth dagger to ask about gross food.

Diesel laughed. "I ate a dung beetle in school. A friend told me it was some magical bug that would help me learn spells faster. That bastard."

"Wait, you had friends?"

Diesel chuckled and elbowed her in the side before pulling out the truth dagger and offering it to her. "You have the next question, my lady."

Despite standing in a stall in the dungeons of Atlantis, Victoria couldn't stop herself from grinning at this ridiculous wizard. She snatched the magical blade from his hands and slid it into his arm. It disappeared into his clothes, and he shivered as it entered. Despite his annoying personality, Victoria was grateful that this blade wouldn't hurt him, at least not physically.

Wait—am I starting to enjoy Diesel's company? She shook the thought from her head. "What was your most embarrassing moment?"

"What a cruel question!" He gave a wounded moan and lifted his hand to his forehead.

She chuckled. "Said the wizard who surprise-stabbed me with a truth dagger."

"*Touché.*"

"Come on, out with it."

His mouth tensed as the words pushed for freedom. "I fell down the stairs at a royal gathering in Fairhaven. There was a huge crowd, and I had to play it off as though an invisible intruder had attacked me."

Victoria burst out laughing. "They believed you?"

"I have my doubts, but at least they played along."

"Oh my God," Victoria pulled out the dagger. She had trouble catching her breath, she was laughing so hard.

He snatched the blade from her and slid it into her side even though she was still convulsed with laughter. "My turn. What was the worst hair cut you ever had?"

Victoria laughed so hard she snorted. "My Mom gave me a china doll cut when I was eight, but she did it herself. Each time she cut one side, it was a little higher than the other. I looked like a boy for almost two months."

He laughed and dropped the truth dagger. It fell to the ground, and Victoria joined it.

She wiped a happy tear from her eye. "You're an idiot, Diesel."

"You love it."

Victoria shook her head and returned the dagger to her pack. "Well, that was...unexpected. I thought you were going to betray me, or make me answer a question I didn't want to."

"Never, my love. Your safety is and always will be my priority."

She rolled her eyes, but smiled all the same. "Thank you."

"Any time." He sat on his half of the straw, which they had separated into two piles, and leaned his back against the wall.

Finally calmer and a bit happier, Victoria was able to settle down. The reality of their situation in Atlantis sank in once more, but this time she could process it with a clear head. "I'm going to take a walk."

"Make sure no one sees you. They'll 'kindly escort' you back here." He closed his eyes and nestled down, getting comfortable.

With a snap of his fingers, the door magically opened.

Victoria smirked at the powerful wizard's gesture. At least they would never truly be locked in this room. She nodded and left, pausing at the door long enough to smile at the sleeping wizard. He was annoying most of the time, but she couldn't help but be grateful he had come.

Victoria sat beside one of the many lakes in Atlantis, elbow resting on her knee as she stared into the deep water and the colorful red koi swimming within it. As much she hated to admit it, Fyrn's warning seemed to be coming true.

Audrey was slipping away.

Victoria smacked the water in frustration and the fish skittered away. *No.* If there was one person Victoria would never give up on, it was Audrey. She knew Audrey better than anyone, and Audrey would never let her down like this. She had quit everything, abandoned everyone else, to join Victoria in her quest for revenge. She had skipped college and a chance at a normal life, all for Victoria.

Audrey had always been there for her.

Victoria stood, smiling with renewed hope. Atlantis had enchanted Audrey, but nothing could steal her away. It was Victoria's job to save her friend, and she would do it even if she had to pull Audrey out of here by the hair, kicking and screaming.

For now, Victoria would wait. Audrey still needed to learn to control her magic and the instructor seemed to be helping, but honestly Victoria wasn't sure they could wait much longer.

More and more, bringing Audrey here seemed like it might have been a mistake.

A nearby flutter of wings caught Victoria's attention, and Styx zipped up to her. She held her hands out so he could drop into her open palms. His tiny chest rose and fell as he gasped for breath.

"Any luck?" she asked.

He shook his tiny head and collapsed into her hands. Victoria couldn't help but think he was milking this a little.

When he had stopped heaving for breath, he hopped onto her shoulder and snuggled into her hair. Even after all their time in Fairhaven, it was still surreal for his tiny hands to pull on her hair as he found a comfy spot.

She headed back toward her stall—she wouldn't be so kind as to call it a bedroom—to find Diesel. They needed a plan.

Shortly after Victoria had left, Diesel had snuck out as well. He had work to do.

Deep in the abandoned tunnels beneath Atlantis, Diesel lifted his staff and shined the light emanating from the crystal at its tip into the depths of yet another abandoned cave. He opened his journal, consulting his notes from the last few tunnels to make sure he understood where he was.

As his light passed along one of the walls, something in the rock began to glow a brilliant red. He paused and examined the ooze, but he didn't recognize it. Carefully, he pulled a small vial out of his bag and took a sample. He could study it when he got home, along with the twenty other samples of various unidentified plants, minerals, and gooey things he had already taken.

Since they'd arrived, he had done nothing but explore and flirt with Victoria. His hosts didn't seem to care for him—a first in Diesel's world, he had to confess—but he couldn't waste the opportunity to discover and learn what he could about their world and culture. It might come in handy later. Besides, it gave him a chance to step away from the utterly distracting Victoria Brie for a bit so that he could get a little work done.

Sometimes he wondered if she had put an enchantment on him, but he didn't care if she had. No one had captivated him like this in almost a decade. She reminded him of young love. It was clear she didn't reciprocate his feelings, but maybe he could wear her down over time. Besides, he got a kick out of the way she rolled her eyes.

He continued down the tunnel, walking for another few minutes before his light exposed a cave-in. Rocks filled the entire tunnel, blocking whatever lay beyond.

He stroked his chin. How strange. The last five tunnels he had explored had ended in cave-ins as well.

Diesel ran his hand along the rocks to look for signs of magical interference or brute strength, and sure enough he saw gouges along the edges of the cave-in, evidence that someone had taken a pickax to the rock and forced it to fall.

Same as all the others.

This was irrefutable evidence that the Atlanteans had purposely cut off most, if not all, their secondary exits. From a logistical standpoint, it didn't make sense to rely on only one entrance and one exit for an entire kingdom of people to escape if need be. He didn't fully understand the logic behind it.

It was fairly clear the Atlanteans didn't want anything getting in... or out.

"But why?" he asked the empty cave.

CHAPTER TWENTY-ONE

Victoria hadn't found Diesel or come up with a plan to rescue Audrey, but she did find a maid who wanted something delivered to Audrey's room.

Just *great*.

Victoria walked down one of the dozens of identical white-walled halls in the Atlantean castle with a dress in her arms and a scowl on her face. Despite the castle's brilliance and the stunning views available from every window, she couldn't get over her anger at the people and just enjoy being in a magical lost city. She fumed, and she couldn't hide it. She had to play her part, at least until—

In her peripheral vision, she saw a guard watching her as she passed. He left his post and followed her, careful to keep his distance but watching her all the same.

The Atlanteans probably didn't want to let a foreigner run unchecked through their castle halls, even if they did just think she was a servant.

Out of spite and stubbornness Victoria picked up the pace, without turning around to let him know she had seen him and knew what he was up to. She wasn't about to let some asshole follow her.

His pace matched hers, and she grinned a bit at the thrill of a chase.

There were probably a hundred hallways in this massive castle, but she at least knew this section of the palace. Up ahead the walkway branched into four halls of bedrooms, council rooms, and what appeared to be a theatre of some sort. There was a deep doorway in the farthest hallway, and she could slip into it to remain unseen.

Using her head start, she rounded the corner and bolted for her hiding place. As she pressed her back against the door, she could hear his footsteps hurrying along the smooth marble floor.

With a smirk on her face, Victoria waited to hear which direction his steps would take. He muttered something under his breath, likely a frustrated curse, and took off down the first hall.

Sucker.

Sure, now it would take a little bit longer to get to Audrey's room, but it wasn't like Audrey would be there. She almost never was. The Atlanteans controlled every minute of Audrey's time in the castle, and allowed her as little time with Victoria as possible.

Besides, it was worth the extra walk to not be followed. To not be watched and treated like an unwelcome guest who couldn't be trusted.

To her surprise, Styx flitted down from the ceiling and trilled in her ear, then tugged on her hair and pointed back to the hall she had just come through. She glanced around, looking for guards or anyone else who might have been watching her, but the hallway was empty.

It seemed like her little pet pixie had found something. *Finally!*

Victoria threw the dress over her shoulder in case she needed it later for an explanation. In this palace it always served her to have a reason to be walking about alone, and "delivering a dress to my master" seemed to be the only excuse that worked.

He darted off down the hall, wings humming through the air. Victoria ran after the pixie, struggling to keep up. Whatever he found had excited him, and he blazed ahead. He darted past a few hallways, but Victoria paused and tensely peeked around each corner to see if there was a guard who would ask her what she was doing. Thankfully these sections of the palace seemed fairly empty, and she was able to run through them quickly.

Styx finally stopped in front of a door identical to the rest and pointed at it, squeaking incoherently. Although the rest were shut and locked, this one stood ajar.

"You clever little thief, you," she said, winking at him.

He grinned and bowed.

As they entered, Victoria was careful to keep an eye out for anyone else lurking about. She had asked Styx to find a vault, so she had been expecting a treasure room filled to the brim with gold and artifacts. Instead she found a boring old meeting room, nothing in it but a table, chairs, although it had a window overlooking one of the brilliant Atlantean lakes beyond the castle.

She set her hands on her hips and quirked an eyebrow at her little pixie. "This isn't a vault, Styx."

He rolled his tiny eyes and pointed toward a wall sconce. She studied it for a moment, not quite sure what he was up to, so he wrapped his arms and legs around it. The silver sconce was thicker than he was, so he struggled to pull it downward. He wriggled and flapped his wings, tongue sticking out the corner of his mouth, and suddenly it clicked for Victoria.

It's a hidden door!

She pulled on the sconce and sure enough, it came down. A door slid silently open, revealing a dark hallway of stacked stone. A thick wooden door with silver hinges waited at the far end.

Styx raced down the hallway and stuck his tiny hand in the lock. His tongue poked from the corner of his mouth again as he focused, staring at the ceiling as his hands maneuvered inside. Seconds later there was an audible click.

Victoria peeked through the now-open door, and a smile spread across her face when she saw gold. Lots and lots of gold.

More important than the gold, however, was the display of items. From daggers and swords to jewelry—even a tiara—the items had been carefully laid on individual white pillows. Though some of the cushions were empty, each had a small note attached to it with a pin. Someone had scrawled on each in a language she didn't understand, and the script reminded Victoria of the language on the map.

"I can't believe I'm saying this, but I need Diesel," Victoria said under her breath.

If she were right, these were the Atlantean Artifacts

Fyrn had mentioned. The notes pinned to each pillow were probably details of what each did, which wouldn't surprise Victoria at all. The Atlanteans carefully controlled everything, and only her advanced training with Fyrn had helped her escape their watchful eye. They probably now believed she was nothing more than a servant, and she wanted to keep it that way.

When others underestimated her, she got the upper hand.

The rumble of men's voices caught her attention and she panicked. She ran to the door and peeked out, but thankfully the door to the meeting room had slid silently shut on its own.

No, the voices were coming from behind the walls.

As she stepped into the hallway, the words became clear. She recognized General Cato's voice, but he was speaking a language she didn't understand.

Even though she didn't understand the native tongue, this was great. All she had to do was get Diesel down here, so he could listen in on the meetings while he deciphered the notes in the vault.

The general's tone changed, his voice deepening, and it sent a chill down Victoria's spine without her understanding why. There was something about this guy—something off—but she didn't know what.

To her surprise, a low and guttural growl escaped Styx. He was staring at the wall through which the voices came, glaring at it as though he were going to strangle someone. He flitted in front of her and put his hands out as if to protect her from some invisible force, but nothing happened. Victoria wondered if the pixie could understand more than just English. It seemed as though he had picked up on something the general had said, perhaps directed toward her.

Shit. She didn't like the idea of him talking about her, especially not if it riled Styx so much. Her instinct told her any feud with this Atlantean general would only end in blood.

She beckoned Styx closer. Careful to keep her voice low, she shared her plan with the pixie. "Keep an eye on the general, but don't let him or any of his minions see you."

Styx saluted.

She wished he could speak English, but he only muttered gibberish. She tapped on her cheek, wondering how he could best be of use. "If our lives are in danger, come boop me on the nose. Okay?"

Styx nodded.

Victoria headed back to the meeting room she had used to enter the vault and pressed her ear against the wall. No voices, thankfully. When she pressed her hands against the door, it slid open. She panicked for a second before confirming that the room was in fact still empty.

Close call.

Apparently just pressing on the door opened it, so she would have to be careful. She darted through the meeting room and slid into the hallway with Audrey's dress in hand, aimed for Audrey's room with a smile on her face.

She still wasn't convinced she should steal, but she could at least learn what they had in the vault. These people weren't allies, and if things devolved they might become enemies. She had to know what powers they possessed.

Plus, if her intuition was right and the general wanted to hurt her or Audrey, Victoria's whole stance on not stealing from them might change.

Luak lounged on an expensive leather couch in an ornate living room filled with golden trinkets and adorned with mahogany crown molding. A little gaudy for his taste, but hey—these people were rich and loved showing off their money. He studied the walls of the mansion, enjoying all the paintings and especially what looked like an original Monet. He bit into an apple, taking the last bite as he examined the gold pendant in his hand. It was covered in red gemstones, and even a soldier like him could appreciate the beauty in the contrast of garnet and gold.

He stood and tossed the core onto the floor before fetching another apple from the fridge. He leaned against the counter and eyed the corpse of the person he had stolen the artifact from, her blood-stained high heeled shoe sticking out from behind the kitchen island. Her corpse lay across the tile floor amidst the pearls from the necklace that had broken in their short-lived battle.

Another Rhazdon Artifact for his master. She would be pleased, especially about this one. His master enjoyed wealth and jewelry, and she had been eyeing this Artifact for some time. He was her favorite Artifact hunter, and for good reason.

He lifted the pendant, trying to recall what it did. He believed this one was about clairvoyance, or maybe it was the one that allowed its host to understand any language.

He couldn't remember, but he knew it was exceptionally powerful.

Perhaps he should keep it.

He cringed almost as soon as he finished the thought, since his master would be furious with him if she knew. Her servants had to wait decades to be allowed additional Rhazdon Artifacts, and they would be given whatever she decreed they were worth.

Luak already possessed several of the best Rhazdon Artifacts in existence, and he wouldn't settle for anything less than perfection. That meant the artifact Victoria had stolen from him.

Soon.

Patience wasn't his strength, but he would have it very, very soon.

CHAPTER TWENTY-TWO

"You continue to impress me, Audrey."

Audrey beamed. She couldn't help but feel pride at her words. She was once again in the palace gardens with her oddly nameless instructor, who had refused to be called anything other than "Miss." Regardless of the odd custom, Audrey relished the warmth radiating from the hidden Atlantean sun as they experimented with more of the artifacts.

Down the red brick path, the bullseye still smoked from a brilliant white blast she had loosed using another Atlantean crystal. They had gone through every single crystal in the display, but Audrey still preferred the power in the first one she had ever used with this instructor.

The instructor returned the crystal to the table. "It astounds me that you were able to use Atlantean magic outside the kingdom, especially with no experience."

"I didn't have a lot of control over it," Audrey said with a shrug.

"I caution you to not dismiss your power so easily.

There is a difference between humility and under-appreciating your talent."

Audrey studied the woman, who in turn watched her with an intrigued expression. They stood in silence for several seconds, Audrey unsure of what to say.

Eventually the instructor smiled. "You have a natural gift, and I hope you continue to use it. I don't believe there's anything more I can do for you, Audrey. It's time for you to advance your studies."

"Can I go out in public and not destroy things? If I left Atlantis, would I hurt anyone?"

The instructor set a hand on her heart, mouth working a bit before she spoke. "I suppose not, but why would you want to leave?"

Audrey couldn't answer. She wanted to share the beauty of Fairhaven's palace and the magical hob glob of creatures living there, but the words wouldn't come. Everything in her core told her to stay here instead, to celebrate the fact that she was special even among the powerful Atlanteans.

After all, hadn't she come home?

Ever since Victoria had ducked her guard the Atlanteans had been far less subtle about the fact that she was being watched. Now two or three followed her everywhere she went, and she hated every step of it.

But with a bit of Diesel's help, the two of them had shed their tail and gotten into the vault unseen.

And man, how she had hated asking for Diesel's help!

"This isn't what I had in mind for our first date, but I'm happy to be spending time with you, my love," the wizard said as he scanned the notes pinned to the various pillows in the vault.

Victoria rubbed her temples. "You exhaust me, Diesel."

"That's an improvement from 'I don't even like you,' so I'll take it." He hummed happily, finger tapping on his chin as he studied the Atlantean Artifacts.

Victoria groaned in annoyance.

Styx flew laps around the massive vault, ducking and weaving around the piles of gold and treasure he was using as his own miniature obstacle course among the fortune that had been stored in here.

"What do they say?" Victoria nodded to the notes pinned beneath each Atlantean Artifact.

Diesel stroked his chin. "They're fascinatingly organized. Every single Atlantean Artifact—and yes, that *is* in fact what these are—has its power listed, along with the spirit or entity attached to it. For those missing from their pillows, a note has been added about who is currently using it."

"Which one does General Cato have?"

"I haven't seen his name on any of these notes yet, but it's inevitable that he has at least one. The queen can charm men to do her bidding, though I find it odd for a regal woman to have seduction powers. I always imagined queens were above such information-gathering methods."

"Hmm. Are there any that give the host immense strength?"

"I haven't seen one yet, but I've only just started. This is too much to remember. I need to write it all down."

He whipped out his journal, but surprisingly didn't use a pen. He stroked his chin again while he studied the pinned notes and ink appeared magically on the paper.

"What's going on?" Victoria examined the book over his shoulder.

He grinned charmingly and leaned in, tilting the book toward her as he took advantage of the excuse to be close. Script continued to appear on the page as Diesel put his arm around Victoria's shoulders. "Neat, isn't it? I came up with this. I never run out of ink, and it's much easier to take notes this way."

"Neat." Victoria smacked him hard across the knuckles and he released her, flinching a bit as he shook out his hand.

"I love it when you play hard to get!"

"Focus, please," Victoria said with an eye roll.

"It will take me a few hours to get everything down," Diesel said. "There's so much information here."

"Make it as quick as you can," Victoria said. They didn't have the luxury of time, and they certainly didn't want to be caught in the vault. With only one exit, they would be sitting ducks.

He nodded and returned to his journal, occasionally checking his notes as he scanned the papers pinned to the pillows.

Victoria paced the room, enjoying the soft flutter of Styx's wings as he flew his laps through the towers of gold coins and piles of jewelry. It was better than silence. Or worse…a conversation with Diesel.

Mostly there was gold. Jewelry, goblets, and piles and piles of gold coins. There were chests overflowing with riches, so Victoria understood why the crime boss Drefus would want to come here. Whoever had this much wealth could live like a king. Hell, they might even be able to *overthrow* a king.

She shuddered at the thought of the crime boss ruling Fairhaven.

To occupy herself Victoria looked in every chest, but found nothing fun—just more of the same. When she had gone through them all, she studied the wall display. Even though she didn't understand what any of them did, she could at least appreciate what they were. Necklaces. Earrings. A few crowns and tiaras. Little white figurines like the ones Audrey had bought in the marketplace. Swords. An axe. She ran her finger along the dagger in her arm.

The seconds ticked into minutes, and the minutes ticked into hours.

"How much longer, Diesel?" Victoria asked eventually.

"I'm almost done. I'm writing as fast as I can, darling."

"Stop calling me—ugh." She didn't bother finishing her sentence.

He grinned.

"Did you find anything that can give me strength yet?"

With a shake of his head, Diesel tapped his finger on an empty pillow. "Some fruity lord has it. We would have to kill him to get it."

Victoria sighed. Not a chance. She wouldn't be like Luak, killing others to take their power.

Too bad.

Voices filtered in and Victoria's heart leapt into her

throat. She ran to the door, summoning her sword just in case, and peeked into the passage.

Empty.

She let out a slow sigh of relief and nodded to Diesel to indicate everything was okay. He resumed his note-taking, but the voices grew louder. She recognized one of them.

General Cato.

Styx fluttered beside her, growling again as he heard the man's voice. Victoria needed to know what he was saying. If it set her otherwise happy-go-lucky pixie on edge, it couldn't be good news.

"Diesel," she whispered.

He looked over, and she gestured for him to join her.

"I'm not done yet," he said, pointing toward the Artifacts.

"This is more important."

He sighed wistfully, looking at the Artifacts for second before joining her. "What is it, my dear?"

Victoria suppressed her usual groan. She needed to focus, even if he wouldn't. "What are they saying?"

Diesel stared at the wall, his eyes going out of focus as he listened. His ears twitched a little, and he nodded to himself. "The general is saying that the king favors Audrey. He's considering adopting her as his heir, because she's powerful and has so much potential."

A pang of loss hit Victoria hard in the chest. In this country, Audrey would be a princess. Talk about temptation!

She swallowed hard, wondering if she could in good conscience ask her friend to give that up. Victoria didn't want to lose Audrey, but she didn't want to stand in her way either.

"The general says they've traced her lineage to some war hero. Even though it's not true the public would believe it, and that would solidify Audrey's rule when she took over."

"Wow," Victoria said softly, running her hand through her hair.

Diesel bristled, face distorting with anger as the men in the next room continued to talk. "Those bastards."

"What?"

"They just want her to rule because she can be controlled. This is the general's attempt to take over the throne. They're saying that the human genes reduce willpower and allow the Atlantean within her to run the show. He's going to control her like a puppet."

Victoria balled hands into fists. "That asshole!"

"Shit," Diesel said.

"Fuck, there's *more*?"

"He's going to tell her to kill us."

Victoria shoulders drooped. "Awesome."

"They're going to give her some special Atlantean Artifact that allows her to change shape, and they're going to make her stay in that form forever. Apparently we make her weak. She's not supposed to treat us as equals, and he thinks her affection for us is holding her back."

"This is bad," Victoria said, pacing the small hallway.

Diesel nodded. "We have to get out of here."

"Let's find Audrey and get out. Tonight. Finish up what you're doing, but we don't have much time."

"How about we, shall we say, *make free* with some of these Atlantean Artifacts?" He flashed her a dazzling grin.

Victoria stood a little taller, looking him in the eye. These assholes were not only planning to manipulate and control her best friend, they wanted Victoria and Diesel dead. They had immense power, an entire army on their side, and an intuitive knowledge of a kingdom Victoria barely knew. She needed every advantage she could find, and while she believed in doing what was right, she also wanted to live. Besides, she didn't care much about stealing from someone who wanted to force her best friend to murder her. "Take whatever you want."

CHAPTER TWENTY-THREE

"Whenever you're ready, Audrey," the king said.

Audrey took a deep breath, but she wasn't nervous. She had spent so much time practicing with the instructor in the gardens that she didn't question the magic in her blood anymore. She knew it would do what she wanted it to do when she wanted it to do it.

The question was merely how much she wanted to show.

For the king, she wanted to give a special performance, provide proof that the time and money he had spent on her while she was a guest in his home had been well worth it. She had mastered the bolts of energy, but there was another technique that took more effort and attention. One that took more skill.

With the artifact in her left hand, she raised her right and summoned the white light from within the stone. It pooled and shimmered in her hand before slowly crawling upward as gentle and elegant swirls of light that she could control. They wafted from her, spinning like ribbon dancers through the air. She was careful not to touch anything with them since they would ignite whatever they touched, just let them be a beautiful display of her power.

The king clapped his hands, a broad smile on his face as he watched the show. "My dear, you have far surpassed what I expected. I am so impressed!"

Audrey smiled, grateful for the recognition. "Thank you for the opportunity to learn."

He caught her eye and beamed like a proud father, which made her stand up straighter with pride. "Audrey, the queen and I have something we would like to share with you tonight. Please be ready for a dinner in your honor and some incredibly exciting news."

"Can you tell me now?" she asked with a mischievous grin.

He chuckled. "I'm afraid not. We will see you tonight."

With that, he bowed his head slightly toward her and exited the throne room, leaving via the route she had seen him and the queen take whenever they left. Their quarters were probably in that direction, but Audrey didn't dare follow.

After all, she was only a guest here.

She headed toward her room, mind buzzing with ideas about what the king and queen wanted to share with her. He had said that he was impressed by her skills, and everyone she spoke to acted like she was here to stay. The thought of her leaving seem to fill them with horror.

After all, she was one of them, and an Atlantean's place was in Atlantis.

When she reached her bedroom, she threw open the double doors and inhaled the sweet air. It was like summer and Christmas rolled into one, and she tasted happiness every time she stepped into this room. The open balcony ushered in another fresh breeze, and she stood on it, hands on the railing, as she stared at the beautiful kingdom. Its lakes glistened in light she still didn't understand, and she had to confess something difficult to herself.

She loved it here, and she didn't want to go.

Audrey fetched her hairbrush from the silver vanity, but her reflection caught her off-guard. Her long dark hair now had the same silky shimmer as every other Atlantean in the kingdom, and though they had only been here two weeks, it had grown a foot. Smiling, blissfully happy, she wove her hair into the same braid she had seen the queen wear and tied it off with a silk string from the vanity.

The door slammed.

Audrey jumped, heart hammering in her chest. It wasn't until she saw Victoria pressed against the closed door that she was able to calm down.

Victoria, however, looked panicked.

"What's going on?" Audrey asked.

"We have to get out of here," Victoria said.

"Why?"

"Diesel and I overheard some dark stuff, Audrey. Our lives are in danger, and we need to go. We need to leave now."

Audrey opened her mouth to speak, concern burning through her at the thought of her friends' lives being in danger. Her instinct was to trust Victoria, since she knew without a doubt that Victoria always told the truth.

But the voice deep in her core disagreed.

She's jealous.

She wants what you have.

She's a threat to everything you've built here.

And the voice was *loud.*

Torn, Audrey fiddled with the crystal in her pocket, and the more she touched it, the more her initial instinct to trust Victoria faded. It was like something took her over, and she believed without a doubt that Victoria was simply wrong.

"I think you made a mistake," Audrey said calmly.

Victoria's face scrunched in confusion. "Diesel heard them talking, Audrey. They want to manipulate you. They're trying to control you."

Audrey shook her head, biting her tongue even as a wave of resentment swamped her. "You didn't hear it for yourself?"

"Well, no. I don't know Latin, or whatever they speak here," Victoria said.

Audrey crossed her arms. "And it never once occurred to you that perhaps you shouldn't make assumptions when you yourself didn't hear what happened?"

"Audrey, I'm serious. This is real, and you're in danger. We all are. We have to get out of here."

Yet again, the instinct to trust Victoria blipped to life in Audrey's chest. She took a step back, trying to make sense of the warring emotions in her body, but in the end her inner voice won the battle. It was as though something came over her, something uncontrollable, and Audrey snapped. "Or maybe you're just tired of not having your own Royal Suite. Maybe you're tired of them mistaking you for a servant. I'm sorry they don't treat you with respect, Victoria, but maybe this isn't about me or Cato or the king. Maybe you're tired of me having the time of my life."

"Audrey, what—"

"You said it yourself that you don't like being here! And yet here I am, finally finding my roots. Finally discovering who I am and what I can do and why I'm powerful, and you want to leave? You want to take that away from me?"

"I'm trying to save you!"

"No, you're just tired of playing second fiddle to me! You think they're treating you like a second-class citizen, Victoria, but that's how I feel every day. No one sees me. No one acknowledges me. No one says anything about what I do to help you. You're the hero, Victoria, and I'm the sidekick. Maybe I don't want to be the sidekick anymore!"

Victoria pointed a finger at Audrey as she closed the gap between them. "You're not a sidekick, Audrey, and you know it."

"Aren't I? I'm ignored back in Fairhaven, but here I'm treated like royalty. Why would I ever leave?"

Victoria's mouth dropped open and she didn't say anything. Neither of them moved for several moments and Audrey's shoulders ached from tension, but she swore to herself she wouldn't back down. She had said what she had never felt safe to say, but now they had emptied their purses on the floor.

Time to see what Victoria would do.

"Fyrn was right," Victoria said softly. With that, she left. The door clicked shut behind her, and the room became painfully silent.

Audrey backed up slowly until she hit a wall, but she still couldn't quite process what she had just said. She almost couldn't remember it, like it had come from someone else. She tugged on the ends of her silky dark hair, baffled by what was going on and simultaneously not wanting to challenge it.

After all, she had a home here.

The impulsive anger faded, replaced by comfort and calm. It felt as though everything were suddenly fine. The memory of her fight with Victoria began to blur, and she couldn't remember anything that had been said. Victoria had been upset—that was all she could recall.

"No," she said, pacing the room. "I want to remember."

Everything is fine, the voice in her core said.

"No it's not!" she said loudly.

Everything is fine, the voice repeated.

Audrey shook her head, still pacing in circles. This wasn't right. It *wasn't* fine. Panic and guilt blurred until she couldn't tell one from the other, and she knew she had to find Victoria. They needed to make this right. Something was happening to Audrey, and she could finally see it. She could finally feel it, and she didn't like it one bit—whatever "it" was. Something was happening to her, and it was more than just her skin shimmering and the silky sheen of her hair. There were other changes going on within her, and those changes would be the death of her if she wasn't careful.

Something clicked for her, and she stopped dead in her tracks.

She and Victoria didn't just need to make things right. They needed to leave.

EVERYTHING IS FINE! the voice shouted within her.

The voice within her was so loud it took her to her

knees. The overwhelming sensation of anger was like invisible hands pushing on her shoulders, trying to pin her to the floor. She fought it, tears burning in her eyes, but her very core shook with fear. Audrey reached out to balance herself, but her palms slid on the polished white marble. Her long dark hair fell onto the cold floor, and she heaved as she tried to catch her breath.

EVERYTHING IS FINE!

The words were a deafening roar both in her ears and in her body. They consumed her, controlled her, taking over every ounce of her willpower and sense of self. They weren't comforting or soothing anymore. Whatever this voice was, it was *assaulting* her. She had to fight.

And she was losing.

EVERYTHING IS FINE!

Within Audrey, something clicked back into place. It was as though a thought pattern had been corrected, or puzzle pieces had been put in the proper order. She stilled, her heart slowing as she tried to remember what she had been so upset about.

It was all fuzzy.

She held her hand to her head and leaned her back against the wall, staring at the ceiling as she tried to make sense of the last few minutes.

She couldn't.

She stood, and suddenly the only thing she could remember was that the king wanted to have dinner with her tonight. Enough nonsense...it was time to get ready. She toyed with the brain in hair, but a worrying sensation pulled on the back of her mind. Something was wrong, but for the life of her she couldn't figure out what.

"How strange," she said softly, the words eerily familiar. She didn't like the sense of déjà vu that came with them, and she wondered what would happen if she ignored the sensation.

At dinner, Audrey found it difficult to eat. She found herself poking at the food with her fork.

"Are you all right, dear?" the queen asked from her seat across the glass table.

Audrey nodded and did her best to smile, but it didn't last long. "I'm fine, thank you. I appreciate you having me for dinner."

The king smiled from where he sat at the head of the table. "I'm sure you're wondering what we want to tell you."

"I'll confess an interest," Audrey said with a chuckle.

The king stood, meat and potatoes still on his plate, and gestured for her to come. She and the queen followed him toward a tapestry behind the table, and he lifted it to reveal a door. It swung inward as they approached, and he led them down a long staircase.

On either side of the stairs were mountains of gold, mainly coins, but also the occasional string of pearls or gemstones. They glittered in the light from the wall sconces, but the king barely seemed to notice them. He led Audrey and the queen toward the bottom of the stairs, where a pedestal awaited them. On the pedestal lay a royal-blue silk pillow with a silver tiara nestled on it, a glimmering clear crystal embedded in its tallest point.

"We wish to invite you to join the royal family and to be my heir," the king said, lifting the tiara and offering it to her.

Audrey couldn't speak at first. She merely reached out with her finger and touched the top of the crown. It radiated power. "This is more than a headpiece, isn't it?"

The king nodded. "You're quite right. This is an Atlantean Artifact, and it will give you the ability to shift into whatever form you want. All you have to do is stay here in Atlantis, and the crown and monarchy are yours."

The voice in Audrey's core spoke for her before Audrey even had a chance to process the offer. "Of course. Nothing would make me happier."

Don't, a tiny voice said in the back of her head. Her smile faltered, and she bit her lip with worry.

What the hell was happening to her?

CHAPTER TWENTY-FOUR

Victoria sat by a pool of water, staring at the koi as they swam in the crystal-clear depths. Even *they* didn't want anything to do with her, and sticking her hand in just chased them away.

Little bastards.

Audrey had never spoken to Victoria like that, and she had seemed genuinely upset. Angry. The sidekick comment had wounded Victoria the most. She hated the thought of her friend feeling like she had been playing second fiddle. Audrey had so much potential, so much grace and power. Victoria couldn't imagine life without her best friend. They had always been there for each other, always had each other's backs.

The thought of leaving Audrey broke her heart.

Victoria frowned, a fresh wave of determination crashing over her. She wouldn't leave Audrey. She *couldn't.* This was the mind control talking. Apparently it had gotten worse than she or Diesel had suspected. Either the general had control of Audrey, or her Atlantean half had taken over.

This wasn't the Audrey Victoria knew and loved.

Victoria stood, determination on her face as she scanned the castle's windows. She would save Audrey from whatever was happening to her, and that meant getting Audrey out of the castle as soon as humanly possible.

Even if it meant dragging her out.

Victoria threw open the door to the room she shared with Diesel. He was stuffing objects into his and Victoria's backpacks, and he paused as she entered. She squared her shoulders. "Diesel, we're leaving. Are you ready?"

"Where's Audrey?"

"We're going to go get her."

Diesel flashed one of his charming grins. "How lovely, darling. A couple's adventure to rescue a friend."

Victoria pinched the bridge of her nose, but ultimately chose to ignore him. "Is everything packed?"

He nodded. "I managed to get us about five Atlantean Artifacts each and hide them in various layers of clothing, so unless we get frisked we should be fine."

"They might look closely."

"Well, let's not give them a reason to," he said with a wink.

"A reason to do what?" a man asked from the door.

Victoria spun around. She hadn't even heard the squeaky door open, and yet it stood ajar. The general leaned against the doorframe, arms crossed, and watched them suspiciously, as though he had caught them red-handed.

Well, he kind of had. *Shit.*

The general pushed off the doorframe and walked toward them with Styx in one hand. The tiny pixie struggled to break free.

Double shit.

"Let him go." Victoria tensed, ready to fight if she had to. Beside her, Diesel tightened his grip on his staff.

The general lazily looked between them, as though they were no threat to him. "I'm not sure how you found it, but our vault contains every known Artifact that has not been given to an Atlantean. All of ours are accounted for, unlike that fool Rhazdon. He let his power disappear into the wind, and that was why he failed. We don't give them to the common folk, as he did."

The general looked Victoria up and down, and her heart skipped a beat.

He knew. She didn't know how, but he knew what she was.

The element of surprise gone, she summoned her sword and attacked. He released Styx and parried, and the two of them dodged and ducked each other's blows in the small room. She threw a blast of energy at the general's head, but he rolled out of the way at the last second and took Victoria down with him. He aimed a punch at her head, but she ducked out of range and his fist broke the stone floor instead. Instead of screaming with pain and nursing broken knuckles, he didn't flinch. He cocked his arm to throw another blow, but she pinned his knee and flipped him over her head. He landed hard on his back.

With a smirk Diesel aimed his staff at the general, the tip burning red, but a blast of energy from the door knocked him onto his back. Suddenly the room was filled with bursts of white light, and Victoria summoned her shield instead of the sword to block them. She ran toward Diesel to give him cover, and he huddled behind the shield with her as he regained his breath. Styx dove toward them and nestled in Victoria's hair.

The general had brought an army, and Victoria didn't have the high ground.

With her free hand, she poked Styx in the belly. "Boop, buddy! You were supposed to boop me on the nose!"

He rambled incoherently, squeaking some defense Victoria couldn't understand.

"It's fine. It's fine, buddy. Stay out of reach, and follow closely if we get caught. We may need you to pick some locks."

He saluted and clicked his heels together before darting into the air.

"Well, damn! That hurt," Diesel said, his voice catching as he held his chest. "I shouldn't have played with my food. I didn't realize he had backup."

Blast after blast ricocheted off Victoria's shield, each magical blow shooting pins and needles up her arm. She grimaced, trying her best to take the hits, but the shield was too heavy. She'd had to summon a massive one to cover them both, and the weight was taking its toll on her. It kept leaning away from her, and she gritted her teeth as she tried to keep it steady. She wouldn't be able to hold it much longer.

Fuck, how she wished she was stronger.

"Looks grim," Shiloh said out of nowhere.

Victoria and Diesel yelped in unison as the ghost appeared out of thin air. He lounged nearby, the occasional bolt of energy sailing through him and singeing the wall.

Diesel's eyes widened with excitement. "Is that the ghost of your Rhazdon Artifact? How fascinating! I have so many questions—"

Victoria interrupted him, grateful for the first time to see her ghost. "Shiloh! Thank goodness. How many of them are there? What's the weapon count? Can we—"

The ghost interrupted her with a massive yawn. He stretched and laid down on the ground as though she hadn't said anything.

"Shiloh!"

"Do you think you'll die?" Shiloh asked, studying his nails as he lounged on the dirty floor.

"Not if you help!"

He peered at something in front of her shield. "Nah."

"Shiloh! *Damn it!*"

As quickly as he had appeared the ghost dissolved into the air. Victoria screamed with frustration.

The blows stopped, and a second later someone kicked her shield *hard*. The sheer force of it threw her against the wall, knocking her head against the stone. Her vision blurred, and the shield disappeared. She fell to the floor, back sliding down the wall. Everything became fuzzy. She knew her name was Victoria, and she was...she was...

Shit, she was *something*. It was on the tip of her tongue.

Blurry silhouettes shouted and danced in her vision, but she couldn't tell what was going on.

Diesel cussed, and a few bursts of light filled the room.

Whatever he was doing, it caused a light show. In her delirious state, Victoria smiled a bit at the brilliant sight. "Shiny."

Someone grabbed her by her neck. It hurt. She gasped for breath and grabbed the massive hand, but her assailant lifted her off the floor. Her head throbbed more painfully now, and she could feel herself slipping toward the darkness. Any second now, she would pass out.

Any second could be her last.

For a moment Audrey could only stare at the scene before her.

She had come to inform Victoria that she was staying, her feet carrying her as though something else were controlling her every step, but she had stopped in her tracks when she saw the army congregated outside Victoria's bedroom.

A gap appeared in the army of Atlantean soldiers, and General Cato walked through. He held Victoria by her neck, her feet dangling in the air as she gasped for breath.

He sneered as he studied his prize, and something within Audrey snapped.

Time slowed, and a rush of memories burned through Audrey's mind. She thought of punching Andy Jones during recess in the third grade because Andy had been picking on Victoria. She remembered their kickboxing classes together, and all the times Victoria had tried to get her to go out for dance or acting or any of the other stupid things that Audrey had no interest in doing but at which

Victoria excelled. She thought of all the car trips, all the near-misses in traffic.

But most importantly, Audrey thought of Victoria's parents dying, of the way Audrey had been the only one Victoria would speak to after her life had imploded. She remembered discovering Victoria's powers in the tree-house, and traveling with her to Fairhaven. She remembered Victoria's squelching feet as she walked through the gas station after destroying a sink with a power she didn't understand.

She remembered *Victoria*.

Audrey staggered as her thoughts cleared. The voice in her core tried to speak, but her newfound clarity silenced it almost instantly.

What the fuck had she been doing? She had nearly let strangers adopt her and shove some magical crown on her head.

Fuck that. Whatever they were doing to her here, Audrey had been inches away from becoming a mindless drone.

And just like that, it clicked for her: that voice in her core was her Atlantean nature, which had fueled an instinctive drive to stay with her people and find purpose. To find community.

But she already had all the community she needed.

"Put her down at once," Audrey said, pointing to the floor for emphasis.

The general jumped in surprise, apparently caught off-guard by Audrey's presence. He simply stared at her for a moment, then his smile faded and he released his grip on

Audrey's friend. Victoria crumpled on the floor in a heap and held her throat, gasping for air.

Victoria might not have been Atlantean, but she was family. In Audrey's mind, that made her an honorary Atlantean, one she would protect with her life.

The general looked disappointed. "They confessed to stealing from our vaults, my lady. They must be punished."

Audrey studied Victoria, who sat still on the floor and watched her, seemingly waiting for Audrey's next move.

Audrey smirked. "I'll take care of punishment. You need not concern yourself with my servants."

Victoria scowled, and Audrey resisted a wicked chuckle at her friend's expense.

The general looked behind him and nodded to one of the soldiers, who disappeared into the bedroom. "Miss Audrey, by now you know you have been chosen to rule, and I promise you that these commoners are a chain around your ankle. They hold you back, my liege."

To her credit Victoria didn't say anything aloud, but her face said it all. She scrunched her nose and grimaced a little, the confused look her equivalent of, "What the fuck is he talking about?"

Audrey again suppressed a smile. "I appreciate your input, general. Dismissed."

He opened his mouth to speak, but Audrey waved her hand to emphasize the fact that she didn't want him to say a word. She nodded down the hall, hands on her hips, and waited in silence for him to obey.

He stood a little taller, frowning. "Should we be concerned about *your* loyalty, Audrey?"

"I prefer 'Your Royal Highness.'"

In Audrey's peripheral vision, Victoria bit her lip to keep from snickering and dropped her head to hide her face.

The general closed the distance between himself and Audrey. He hesitated, letting the tension settle in the air as his eyes roamed her face. "Perhaps you did not hear me, Your Royal Highness, but these commoners snuck into our vaults and stole some of our most precious possessions— Atlantean Artifacts. Either they used their influence with you to steal from us, or you distracted us long enough to let them do so. Which is it?"

Audrey's lips parted. Honestly, she didn't know what to do. "I'll handle punishment. Thank you, General."

He grabbed her hand, and though she expected it to be rough, his grip was gentle. His calloused finger rubbed the skin on her wrist and he didn't break eye contact. His expression softened from anger to concern, and a flicker of understanding crossed his face.

"It seems you've woken up," he said so softly that only she could hear.

She tensed, and his grip on her wrist tightened until she couldn't move. "Let go of me, Cato."

He shook his head. "It won't take much to fix this, and I promise you'll be happier for it. Come with me."

He dragged her down the hall, and the small army of soldiers followed behind them.

Like hell.

Audrey twisted her wrist in his grip as she had learned in kickboxing and broke free. Without missing a beat, she lifted her skirt enough to kick out his knee. He fell to the ground and the soldiers behind her glanced at one another, apparently not entirely sure what they were supposed to do.

"Grab her!" the general shouted.

"Release them!" she commanded.

The soldiers focused on her, and several crept closer.

Oh, well. It had been worth a try.

Audrey tensed, settling into a defensive stance as she prepared to fight. She wished Victoria would stand up and Diesel would appear from wherever he was hiding, but it seemed like they had already been beaten. If the soldiers could take Victoria, Audrey didn't stand a chance.

Didn't mean she wouldn't try.

The first soldier reached her, and she landed a blow in his solar plexus. He gasped for breath, and she kicked him onto his back as the next soldier arrived. She repeated the blows, and that soldier fell too.

Beside her, Victoria lurched to her feet and summoned a sword. She could barely stand, and from the way she rocked as she swung it was obvious she'd hit her head pretty hard. She didn't have much balance, but she still took out two soldiers with a single swing. One of the men shot a bolt of white lightning at her, but she ducked out of the way with seconds to spare. The motion sent her to the floor, however, and she struggled to get to her feet again.

What had these fuckers *done* to her?

Time to bring out the big guns.

In one hand Audrey held the magnificent artifact given to her by the instructor in the gardens. She stretched the fingers of the other and released the white energy she had practiced with. While she wanted to use the ribbon dancers, as she called them, they would require too much focus at the moment. She needed something quick and effective. She loosed a massive bolt of white energy, hitting every standing soldier in the chest. They tipped over like pins in a bowling alley, crashing to the floor.

Score.

Of course, an attack that strong left her breathing heavily, and she didn't know when she would have enough moxie to attack again.

Time to bail.

"Victoria, let's go!"

"Audrey, look out!" Victoria screamed.

A bolt shot past Audrey, singeing the wall, and she spun on her heel. The general aimed for her head and she ducked just in time, rolling along the floor as the attack flew over her. Her legs caught in her dress, though, and she skidded the last half of the way. Another bolt headed toward her, and she barely pulled her shoulder out of its path. She aimed a bolt at his chest, the easiest target, but it came out as a thin line rather than the full attack she had hoped for. He flinched as though she had thrown a stone at him, nothing more.

Crap.

He chuckled darkly. "You need to build stamina, Audrey. No worries, I'll train you."

Nearby, some of the soldiers were trying to stand. Though the ones closest to her blast still lay steaming on the floor, those who had been behind the front lines were struggling to their feet. They would probably be back in action soon.

Victoria pushed herself to her feet and swung her sword at the nearest one, slitting his throat. He screamed and fell while Victoria aimed for the next soldier, and the next. Audrey knew she would keep going until she couldn't move anymore, but judging by the way she staggered between each blow it wouldn't be much longer.

Audrey wanted to help her, or better yet tell her to go sit down, but her own hands were full. Two soldiers attacked her after the general's bolt missed, one grabbing her shoulders and pulling her back as she kicked the other in the groin. The wounded one fell to his knees, clutching himself, but the other wove his arms through hers and locked them behind her head. She clawed for his hair, his eyes—anything to give her the upper hand—but he held her still.

Three of the guards with a clear shot aimed their white energy beams straight into Victoria's chest. She grunted, jaw tight as though she were being electrocuted, and fell to the floor seconds later. Her sword clattered to the ground and disappeared in a puff of smoke.

"Victoria!" Audrey yelled, looking for a reaction. Victoria was so still she might have been dead.

But she couldn't be dead. Victoria would never leave Audrey hanging like that.

The general watched Audrey struggle with the soldier, and he shook his head. "We can't have this behavior from the princess."

"I'm not your princess," Audrey spat.

"You will be." He put his hand flat against her abdomen and lifted a white crystal like the one she had been training with in the gardens.

Oh, Shit. This would hurt.

Electricity pummeled her, and her jaw tightened until it

squeaked. Her fists clenched, and her body hummed. Worst of all was the pain. It was as though tiny creatures were slowly ripping apart every muscle in her body, but she could do nothing to stop them.

The general removed his hand and Audrey crumpled in the soldier's grip. She tried to stand, but her shoe slid on her long skirts.

These assholes had even gotten her to wear skirts. She was the Jeans Queen. She hated dresses and anything with frills. If they had been able to make her wear gowns, she had been closer to losing herself than she had realized.

The general grabbed her arm and led her down the hallway, and her slippered feet shuffled to keep up.

"You know what to do," the general said to one of the soldiers.

The solider lifted Victoria and the company marched down the hall, two more soldiers carrying an unconscious Diesel between them. Victoria blinked herself awake and caught Audrey's eye, and a surge of relief crashed through Audrey despite the terrible situation.

Victoria wasn't dead. Yet.

Audrey did her best to hide her panic. She grimaced, using their unspoken gestures to ask for help. *What I do?*

Victoria slowly shook her head. *No idea. I'm thinking.*

The general tugged on Audrey's arm, yanking her forward until she couldn't see Victoria anymore. Her mind raced to come up with a plan, but she had spent every waking moment since arriving in Atlantis in the castle. She didn't know the kingdom, or even how to leave except through the main entrance where they had come in, and it was unlikely the king and queen would just let her walk through the door.

"Unhand me!" she shouted, doing her best impersonation of a spoiled princess.

"I will, as soon as you remember who you really are," the general said ominously.

Audrey peered over her shoulder one more time, but Victoria was gone. The last few soldiers in the column marched down an earlier hallway as the general led her down another.

"If you kill them I will make your life a living hell," Audrey said, glaring at the general.

He spun her around and pressed her against the wall, scowling at her. "You don't threaten me, princess. Your life was planned the minute you walked into the kingdom. You *will* take the crown, you *will* transform into an Atlantean, you *will* rule, and you *will* marry me so that I can finally be king."

"Jesus, could your plan be anymore cliché?"

His jaw tensed, and Audrey figured he was debating whether to hit her. *Bring it.* She could take it, and it would just make her hate him more. It would fuel her fire.

Instead, he released her and set a hand on the back of her neck. With his powerful thumb poking into her jaw, he guided her down the hallway. She tried to wriggle out of his grip, but his fingers pressed into her spine. She winced, walking forward to avoid the pain.

This wouldn't last. She, Victoria, and Diesel would get out of here. And if the general hurt a hair on Victoria's head, Audrey would kill the motherfucker.

CHAPTER TWENTY-FIVE

The general pushed Audrey ahead of him as they walked through another dark tunnel. This was more like a cave than any part of the castle. Audrey didn't have a clue where they were anymore. This place seemed to be filled with secret doors and passageways, which would've been cool in any other circumstance.

"So what's the plan, General?" she asked the Atlantean behind her.

He put his hand on the small of her back, but she pushed him off her. Her body still ached from his attacks, and she didn't have the strength to do anything more than bat his hand away. To his credit, he didn't try again. "You'll see."

She rolled her eyes. "I assume you're taking me to the tiara."

It was a solid assumption and the general's eyebrows shot to his forehead in surprise, confirming she was right. It made sense, after all. She assumed there was some kind of controlling aspect to the tiara, and he would want her to wear it sooner rather than later to keep her under his thumb.

That wouldn't happen.

General Cato led her into a massive underground cavern with stalactites covering the ceiling, reaching toward them like teeth. A platform had been carved into the floor, and on it was an ornate silver altar, long enough for a person to lie on.

Surprisingly, the king stood behind the altar with his arms behind his back and a disappointed expression on his face.

"After all we've done for you," he said softly, shaking his head.

Audrey curtsied mockingly. "Thank you for your hospitality. I wasn't aware kidnapping your guests and forcing them to stay was customary."

The king clicked his tongue. "You will not speak to me that way."

"I just did." Audrey quirked an eyebrow, daring him to do something about it.

Sure, Audrey might have been walking a line here, but she didn't have many cards to play. For whatever reason they still wanted her to be their little princess, and if she could distract them long enough Victoria might be able to escape and get them all out of here.

The king snapped his fingers, and the small army dragged in a struggling Victoria and an unconscious Diesel.

Audrey sighed and resisted the impulse to face-palm. So much for her plan.

She eyed the king. Usually he wore a long cloak which

hid his shoulders and much of his body. Tonight, though, he'd gone without. His barrel chest and broad shoulders reminded her of an MMA fighter, and she wondered how strong an Atlantean had to be to be king. He could probably beat the general in a fistfight, and since she had just lost to Cato she doubted she could take them both.

Brute force wasn't going to win this war or get her and her friends out safely. She needed to be clever.

A realization hit Audrey. "I don't remind you of your dead children, do I?"

The king shook his head. "The queen and I have never had children, nor will we. Everything we did was done to woo you."

"How ethical."

The king placed his hands behind his back again. "Enough of this, Audrey. You must choose to either be an Atlantean and live with us, or spend your final moments as a commoner and die with your servants."

"Great choices," she mumbled.

The king shook his head patronizingly. "Either way, they die tonight. You don't have to. Only Atlanteans may know of our great city. Surely you understood that? This law keeps us safe. Your servants' deaths were inevitable. You've had your fun, so choose!"

The soldiers dropped Victoria and Diesel at the foot of the platform, and Diesel's eyes snapped open. He scanned the cave, his hand searching his chest for something, and he looked panicked. His mouth eventually settled into a fine, grim line, and he stared at Audrey as if waiting for her to act.

The king snapped his fingers, and a servant girl brought

a pillow with the tiara on it. The king lifted the headpiece and walked toward her, every step slow and precise as he held her gaze. "This is an Atlantean Artifact, remember, one that will be your eternal tie to the city. To fuse with it, you must sacrifice something precious to you. I recommend you sacrifice them." He gestured toward Victoria and Diesel.

Audrey needed a plan, but her mind kept drawing blanks. Perhaps she could pit the two Atlantean men against each other. "The general is playing you—"

"I know," the king said with a dismissive wave of his hand.

"What?" The general and Audrey said in unison.

"You've wanted to rule for decades, Cato. I assumed you fabricated the story about Audrey's heritage, but it's of no matter to me. You'll rule if and when I let you. For now, I want my heir. Audrey, come."

Shit. That plan hadn't worked either.

Audrey's curiosity got the better of her. "Why me? You have a kingdom full of full-blooded Atlanteans but you want some human hybrid?"

The king smirked, his eyes narrowing, and a chill shot clear to Audrey's toes. "Yes, I want a hybrid. I can program you to do whatever I desire. Your blended nature is powerful and gives you better access to the Atlantean magic in your blood, but you're emotionally weak, Audrey. That's the human in you. You want to please, and your willpower will fail over time. You will obey me, and you won't have a choice in the matter. You won't remember this conversation. By the time I'm done with you, you won't even remember those commoners you came here with, much less your life before Atlantis. Now, girl, come here."

Mind racing, Audrey hesitated. Her impulse was to punch him in the gut, but that would most likely backfire. To stall for time, she reached for the tiara. As her fingers touched the glistening metal, the Atlantean voice within her shrieked with joy. It wanted her to put it on, and she felt the familiar tingling numbness that had come every time she listened to it. This time she would not surrender to the voice.

But the king didn't know that.

"It is beautiful," she said in her best imitation of a mindless drone. She tried to sound airy and dazed. Hopefully he would take the bait.

"It is," the king said softly.

Her heart thumping, Audrey lifted the crown to examine it in the light, using the opportunity to cast a wary glance toward Victoria. As their eyes connected, Victoria smirked.

Good. She knew what Audrey was trying to do. Hopefully Victoria could get them out of here, because Audrey was plumb out of ideas.

Victoria knew that expression on Audrey's face. It was clear panic. *Help me.*

Victoria subtly pointed toward the king. *Stall them.*

Audrey nodded slowly, disguising the motion by tucking her hair behind her ear.

It was everything Victoria could do to not let out a sigh

of relief. She had been so afraid she had lost her friend, but something had happened back in the hallway to wake Audrey up.

Thank God. Now, to get out of here…

The king paced around Audrey, his hands behind his back. "It may cause you pain to kill them, dear, but your rewards will be great. You will have a public that adores you. You will have a kingdom at your feet. You will have a home."

At that Audrey froze, her eyes glazing over just a little as she stared at the tiara.

Shit, Victoria didn't have much time. Whatever they had done to brainwash her before, it looked like maybe it was working again.

The stubborn warrior in Victoria wanted to stay and run her sword through them all, but she couldn't. The frustration of not being strong enough to wield her sword and shield at the same time weighed on her. She had all this power available, but she didn't have the strength to use it.

They would have to run.

Styx flitted from boulder to boulder nearby, staying out of sight. He paused on one and stared at her, probably waiting for orders.

"Stand down," she mouthed to him.

He nodded his tiny head and retreated to the shadows.

"What do we do?" Diesel whispered in her ear. He had snuggled against her, but she didn't have time to care that he had taken advantage of yet another inappropriate moment to steal a bit of intimacy.

She leaned her forehead against his as though she were a frightened lover, using the proximity to plan their escape.

"I don't know. Can you cook up a magic portal to get us out of here?"

"Yeah, but it's illegal and highly dangerous."

Victoria couldn't help herself. She quirked an eyebrow and studied him, trying to tell if he was joking. "I was kidding, but are you serious?"

He nodded. "I need my staff, but I can do it."

"Where is it?"

"That asshole has it," Diesel nodded toward one of the soldiers in the back, who leaned on Diesel's staff as though it were just a piece of wood he had found in the forest and not a powerful magical artifact. The soldier examined his nails, not even paying attention to the forced coronation on the platform before him. Maybe this was standard fare for Atlantis.

Hell, it probably was. This place had its fair share of crazy.

"How much energy do you have to fight?" Diesel whispered in her ear.

"Enough." Victoria's muscles ached, but at least she wasn't dizzy anymore. She could see straight again, and she didn't feel as though she were having the life choked out of her. A migraine squeezed the back of her head and lights danced in her vision, but the Rhazdon Artifact was healing her already. She would be fine in just a few minutes. She could even take a few more blows to the chest from that white energy the Atlanteans loved using, but each time one hit she ran the risk of it worsening her pulsing migraine.

"Cover me, then," Diesel said. He jumped to his feet, and Victoria followed suit. She summoned her shield and threw herself into the crowd of soldiers. They crumpled beneath her, and she put all her energy into making the shield as heavy as she possibly could. At least ten of them were trapped beneath it, and she struggled as the massive weight pulled on her arm. She tried to move with it, but a few of the other soldiers who had escaped the blow attacked her from behind.

On the platform, the king rolled up his sleeves, shaking his head. "When you want something done right—"

"Do it yourself," Audrey finished for him. She reached into the general's pocket and pulled out the glistening white crystal he had stolen from her, then kicked him squarely in the chest. He shot over the side of the platform and skidded on the floor. Seconds later, Audrey released a hail of white lightning at the king.

The energy hit the king's chest and he sailed in the opposite direction as the general, skidding across the floor and hitting his head hard on a protruding boulder.

Victoria released the shield and it disappeared. She jumped to her feet and drew her sword, slashing at the Atlanteans stupid enough to attack her. They were inching in on either side of her, several of them preparing a white energy attack. She needed to get to better ground. A gap appeared between her and the altar, so she bolted for it to distract them from Diesel's rescue attempt on his staff.

A hail of white light shot around her as the guards attacked, but she ducked behind the altar and pulled Audrey behind it as well with seconds to spare. The energy burned the altar's ornate legs and seared into the carved platform.

Bursts of green light cut through the soldiers just then, and several of the men screamed. The ground shook, and

Victoria risked a peek around the altar to find Diesel in the middle of the cavern, the soldiers around him unconscious on the floor.

Victoria quirked an eyebrow. "That'll do."

He ran toward them as one of the soldiers stumbled to his feet to give chase. Unfazed, Diesel aimed his staff at the Atlantean and let loose a green blast of light that hit the soldier so hard he flipped.

In seconds Diesel skidded behind the altar, and Victoria grinned. "Nice work."

"Ready to leave?" Diesel asked.

Audrey nodded violently. "Get me out of this place."

Diesel chuckled and extended his hands, face furrowing with focus. "I need you to take care of anyone who tries to distract me. I have to do this exactly right, or we could all die."

"Oh, no pressure," Victoria said. She drew her sword and peered around the altar, where she saw several of the guards starting to stand up.

A blast of white light nearly hit her in the head, but sizzled against the altar inches away instead.

The general stood barely ten feet from the platform, a scowl on his face as his extended hand filled again with white light.

"Anytime, Audrey," Victoria said, tapping her friend on the shoulder.

"Me? You're the hero here."

"Let's fight fire with fire. Shoot another white magic thingy."

"I don't have any 'white magic thingies' left! I need a minute."

"What—goddamn it!" Victoria summoned her shield and made it as large as she could, resting it against the altar for support as its massive weight pulled on her shoulder yet again. Barely a second later a blast of energy hit her shield. She clenched her teeth and did her best to hold the fort.

"Just a little bit longer," Diesel said, voice straining.

"Any day would be great!" Victoria shouted.

"Come on!" Audrey shouted.

Someone grabbed Victoria's shoulder and dragged her backward. The shield disappeared as her focus wavered, and the last thing she saw in the cavern was the general's scowling face.

CHAPTER TWENTY-SIX

Victoria hit the hard ground with a *thunk* and something in her arm snapped. Agony shot down her back as she cradled it and backed away out of instinct.

She had no idea what was happening.

Heart thudding in her chest, she took in her surroundings. They were in some kind of cavern, though it wasn't as large as the one with the altar and was thankfully devoid of any soldiers or bloodthirsty kings. Water dripped slowly from a few stalactites on the ceiling. She could hear only her ragged breathing in the otherwise-still cave, and the sensation made her feel as though she had disrupted a tomb.

"Shit," Diesel said.

Victoria peered over her shoulder to find a portal in one of the walls, its edges glimmering gold and pulsating. When she looked through the portal the altar obstructed most of her view of the stumbling Atlantean soldiers. A few regained their balance more quickly than the others and rushed toward her.

Styx bolted through the portal, a panicked expression on his face as he shot straight for Victoria's hair. Once safely in it, he trembled.

"Shh, you're okay," Victoria whispered. His shaking stilled, but he didn't leave the hair-fortress.

"Close the portal!" Audrey shouted.

Diesel grabbed his staff off the ground and pulled Victoria to her feet. "I can't! I screwed up. It will close on its own in a few seconds. We should run."

Victoria groaned and reached for Audrey, pulling her friend to her feet before they raced down the nearest tunnel. "Where are we, Diesel?"

"Fairhaven, deep in the tunnels below. It'll take us hours to get up there. Any Atlantean stupid enough to follow us will get lost down here and hopefully eaten by something."

"Hopefully *we* don't get eaten by something!" Exhausted, Victoria struggled for breath as they ran. The Rhazdon Artifact in her arm thankfully healed her shoulder, and a surge of relief followed the cessation of pain. She could breathe more easily now.

A burst of white light sailed past Victoria's head. The general was standing in the tunnel, seething. His shoulders heaved, and more white energy burned in his hand. Four soldiers stood beside him, their hands lifted and filled with white light as well. Thankfully, though, the portal had begun to close. It was only wide enough for perhaps a hand to get through, and it finally sealed.

Cato was a powerful man who could probably kill them all, and Diesel had been foolish enough to give him a backstage pass into her city. The fight would continue, but now it was in her backyard. "Diesel!"

"I had limited time, darling!" the wizard said, exasperated. "Portals are incredibly complex!"

She frowned, more annoyed with herself than Diesel. General Cato couldn't have won against Victoria in Atlantis if she had been strong enough to wield her Rhazdon Artifact properly. She gritted her teeth and skidded to a halt. "We can't let this guy into Fairhaven!"

Audrey skidded to a halt beside her, as did Diesel. He gestured down the tunnel. "The creatures down here will eat him. If you're really worried, you and I can go for reinforcements, at least. Prepare for him up top."

Another blast of light sailed by Victoria, but she ducked it easily. "And risk innocent lives? No, Diesel. We end this here."

He hesitated, but ultimately sighed in defeat. "Anything you ask of me, my dear snickerdoodle."

Victoria rolled her eyes at the new pet name. That was new and not altogether welcome, but at least he wasn't fighting her on this. "I'll go after the general. Diesel, you take out the soldiers. Styx, you stay out of harm's way."

Styx bolted out of Victoria's hair and hovered in front of her face, pouting.

"I'll be okay," she said with a smile.

He booped her on the nose and flew toward the ceiling, out of attack range.

Victoria watched her little buddy fly to safety and sucked in a deep breath to steady her racing heart. "Audrey, you rest behind cover until you're ready. I'm going to need your help as soon as you can give it."

Audrey nodded and ducked behind a boulder as the general released a blast of light. It radiated from him like a tsunami, so Victoria summoned her shield. She had to kneel to make one big enough to protect both her and Diesel. The attack battered her shield, shooting pins and needles through her arm, but she held her ground.

As the blast faded, Diesel snuck a kiss onto her cheek and rolled out into the cavern. She shook her head, fighting back a scathing remark so that she could focus. She had a corrupt general to kill.

As bursts of green light from Diesel's staff sailed toward the soldiers she attacked the general, releasing the shield and summoning her sword as she swiped for his neck. He ducked out of the way, but only barely. He lifted his hand to attack her and she summoned her shield again, falling to her knees as the bolt hit. Even though she took a few seconds to let the Rhazdon Artifact heal her, he had hurt her worse than before. For the first time it didn't feel as though she was healing fast enough.

They danced like this for what seemed like forever, Victoria getting more and more exhausted with every shift between the shield and the sword. She wished she could hold them both at once.

Hell, she had to try.

Throwing Fyrn's warnings to the wind, she summoned one to each hand. The shield was small, barely enough to protect her torso and head, but it did the trick. Her sword looked duller than usual, barely glinting any light at all, but it had appeared on cue.

A first. She wanted to giggle with joy.

General Cato yelled and lobbed another blast of energy toward her, so alas—she couldn't relish her success any longer. She ducked, and every fiber of her being screamed at her to drop both weapons.

It wouldn't take much. All she had to do was get in close enough to deal a deadly blow.

Hang in there, Victoria, she thought to herself.

Blood covering his face and neck from their battle, the general charged her. He looked exhausted, running on fumes and ready to keel over, so Victoria took advantage of the moment. He cocked a fist and aimed for her jaw, but she ducked and fell to one knee. With all her might, she yelled a battle cry and thrust her sword at the general, catching him in his gut.

But the blade was too dull to cut him open.

Although she had succeeded in bringing both to her hands, her weapons were weaker. They dissolved in a wave of exhaustion, and she fell to her knees with nothing to protect her. The general kicked her in the chest and she sailed backward along the cavern floor.

She groaned in agony, her body screaming at her to lie still even when she knew she couldn't afford to. Adrenaline pumped through her veins, but it wasn't even enough to help her stand up, much less summon the dark magic in her blood.

The bloody general limped toward her, summoning more of the white energy into his hand. The blindingly white electricity fizzed and popped more violently than before. Victoria backed away, trying to stand, but her feet gave out underneath her.

This couldn't be happening. Victoria couldn't lose, not to some asshole from a kingdom she didn't care about. She had to kill Luak. She wanted to see Fairhaven again. She needed to avenge her parents.

She couldn't die. Not yet. Not here. Not by *his* hand.

Audrey still didn't have much of her energy back, but she bristled when the general kicked Victoria to the ground. He lifted his hand, aiming for Victoria's head, and Audrey knew what would happen next. He would unleash a massive bolt, one from which not even Victoria could recover.

Audrey had to stop this.

She held the beautiful crystal in her hand, willing it to give her everything it had, and she aimed the full force of the blow between his eyes. She aimed her fingers like a gun and lowered her thumb to imitate firing a shot. The white light sailed from the pointer finger, sharp and focused, and it hit right on the mark. General Cato flew backward at least twenty feet, sliding along the ground until his head smacked against a boulder.

Not far away, Diesel shot a blast of green energy clear through the chest of the last soldier who had made it through the portal. The soldier fell to his knees and slumped onto the ground, a hole sizzling between his shoulder blades.

Audrey ran to Victoria, but Victoria waved her away. "Finish him."

The general groaned, rolling onto his side, but Audrey wasn't going to let him get up again. She ran to him and towered over him, lifting the tiara and setting it on her head. "How do you like your princess now?"

With that Audrey fired again, and the bolt of white light hit him square in the middle of the forehead.

Agonizing and unbelievable pain rippled through Audrey from her forehead to her toes. She screamed, unable to control herself, and collapsed to the ground.

Her world went dark. Her only sensation was the steady ringing in her ears, as though she had stepped on a landmine and gone deaf. She struggled to feel her body—to feel *anything*—but she couldn't.

In the darkness, a gentle blue light appeared like blood pooling on a fingertip after a pin pricks it. The little blip of light slowly morphed into a moving figure, like a tadpole swimming back and forth. Audrey squinted, trying to make sense of what was happening, and the light morphed into a giant koi that swam through the air around her. The blue fish brushed her skin, its soft scales leaving a trail of glittering light behind.

I am a water spirit, the fish said without moving its lips. That soft voice echoed in her mind, as gentle as ripples in a pond.

"I'm Audrey," she said. At least, she tried to. She couldn't feel her mouth or hear her words.

I know, sweet thing. You are safe. I am the spirit of your Atlantean Artifact, and I believe we will be great friends.

"But Atlanteans are evil," Audrey managed to say.

The fish chuckled, the sound like water dripping into a pond. *Life is not so simple, dear one, as to be simply divided into good and evil. I will never hurt you, but you will learn this for yourself. I hope you will come to trust me, as we'll be together for quite some time. Now, wake.*

"Audrey!" someone screamed. Someone familiar.

Victoria.

CHAPTER TWENTY-SEVEN

Victoria lifted Audrey by her shoulders, resisting the impulse to shake her friend awake. She lay still as death on the ground, as though something had knocked her unconscious.

"Audrey!" Victoria screamed. "Don't you dare fucking die!"

As if on cue, Audrey gasped and opened her eyes. They darted around, unable to focus on one thing for very long as she got her bearings. She reached out and grabbed Victoria's arm, the panicked grip painfully tight.

"Oh, thank God," Victoria said, pulling Audrey into a hug.

"What happened?" Audrey asked, blinking rapidly as she finally focused on her friend's face.

"You fused with the Atlantean Artifact," Diesel said. He leaned against his staff, studying her forehead.

Audrey reached for her forehead, and sure enough, she was met with cold metal. The tiara's metal had melted into her skin, and as her finger ran along the edge it became difficult to tell where it began and her skin ended. "Oh, shit! No, no, no, no! This is bad. Are they going to control me? What am I going to do?"

Diesel shook his head. "Calm down. You're fine. I don't think the Atlantean Artifact will allow them to control you, Audrey. From what I understand the king was referring to controlling you through other means, possibly food and brainwashing. I think the Atlantean Artifact was merely supposed to make you look like them. After all, that's what it does, isn't it? It allows you to change form?"

Audrey frowned. "How did you know that?"

Victoria nodded toward the wizard. "Mister Many Languages here was deciphering the notes in one of their vaults that had all the Atlantean Artifacts. I assume this one was missing?"

Diesel nodded. "The description mentioned that it was a tiara and its power involved shapeshifting. You can become anything you want, from ogre to Atlantean. I assume they wanted you to use it to look like them and fit in."

Audrey grinned. "No thanks."

Victoria tapped her chin and examined the Atlantean general's corpse, not altogether comfortable with how little she cared about looking at a dead body. Fairhaven had certainly changed her. "Diesel, what was the general's Atlantean Artifact? He was incredibly strong."

Audrey's eyes widened. "Do you think…"

Victoria cautiously nodded, trying not to get her hopes up. If he had an Atlantean Artifact that could make him stronger, maybe she could take it.

Diesel sighed in disappointment. "I'm sorry, my love, but he didn't have one."

"What?" Victoria set her hands on her hips, not believing what Diesel had said. "But he's the general of the Atlantean army. Or, well, he was until we killed him."

Diesel shrugged. "I don't understand either. I went through every note on every pillow in that vault. His name wasn't listed. If he has an Atlantean Artifact, it's not one that was written down. Since even the king's and queen's were written on the parchments, I doubt General Cato had one. It seemed as though he and the royal family were at odds, so perhaps the king didn't trust the general with one even as he was promoted through the ranks. Maybe he was testing Cato in some way before giving him one. We may never know."

"I certainly don't want to go back to find out," Audrey muttered.

Victoria slumped her shoulders in defeat, trying not to be disappointed. Technically, they had gotten what they went into Atlantis to find: instruction for Audrey. Judging by her performance in their small battle, Audrey had finally begun to control her Atlantean magic. In the end, that mattered most.

Victoria pulled her friend into a hug. "I'm glad to have you back."

"But how did I fuse with the artifact? I had to give up something valuable, and I didn't care about that jackass at all." Audrey pointed toward the general's body and the smoke sizzling from between his eyes.

"I believe it was more what he represented," Diesel said.

Victoria nodded. "Audrey, you sacrificed a kingdom.

Fame. Adoration. You sacrificed everything an Atlantean craves in life. And most importantly, you sacrificed a family. The king may have had shady motives, but he wanted to give you the throne."

Audrey smiled. "But *you* are my family."

Victoria beamed. She couldn't help it. She pulled Audrey into another hug, and this time Diesel joined them. Victoria laughed, pushing the wizard away, but he was relentless. She finally allowed it, relishing the peace and quiet.

They had done it. Not only had they rescued Audrey, but they had saved Fairhaven from a threat no one had known existed.

"Let's go home," Victoria said.

As they trudged through the tunnels beneath Fairhaven, Victoria was careful to stay beside Audrey. She wanted to be there in case her friend experienced any aftereffects from fusing with the Atlantean Artifact.

Victoria nudged Audrey in the shoulder. "Back in Atlantis, you mentioned you felt like my sidekick. Do you remember that?"

Audrey stumbled and ran her hand through her hair. "Yeah, vaguely. Sorry. Our conversation is mostly a blur, but I do recall that line."

Victoria shook her head. "Don't apologize, I understand. I'm sorry you felt that way, but now that you're a host as well, you'll know firsthand what it's like. You'll see for yourself that being a host isn't all it's cracked up to be."

Audrey rolled her eyes. "Being adored is hard?"

Victoria almost corrected Audrey. She almost went into a diatribe about how people looked at her with fear most of the time. Being a Rhazdon host meant she was under constant threat of being killed, and even some of the people she saved didn't appreciate or trust her.

Maybe she was wrong. Maybe Audrey would never know what that was like. The Rhazdon and Atlantean Artifacts were different, after all.

But should Audrey become adored by the city, Victoria would never want to take that from her. She kept silent, walking through the tunnels toward Fairhaven, determined to let Audrey have her fun for as long as it would last.

CHAPTER TWENTY-EIGHT

After a while, the tunnels became familiar to Victoria. She recognized the paths Fyrn had taken when they went to their secret training cave, and it wasn't long before she could lead the way to Fyrn's cottage.

"Hopefully he's there," Victoria said, picking up the pace. Styx sat on her shoulder, asleep in her hair.

"Tired of me already, my love?" Diesel asked, a hand on his heart as if wounded.

Victoria rolled her eyes. "We need to talk to him about Audrey's Artifact. She needs to learn how to use it."

Audrey chuckled. "Or I could just take a freaking break, Victoria. I could use about a month of sleep right now."

Again Victoria bit her tongue. A Rhazdon host couldn't rest, but maybe an Atlantean one could.

As they emerged from the tunnel, Fyrn's cottage came into view. The lights were off, and no smoke spewed from the chimney. "Dang. Not home."

The fluttering of wings above them startled Victoria and she tensed in preparation for an attack. Instead, a little blond fairy girl flitted toward them. "You must go to Bertha's at once through the secret tunnels. You must not be seen!"

Victoria hesitated. "Why?"

Diesel grabbed her arm and pulled her back into the tunnel, alert and suspicious. "That's one of Fyrn's messengers, Victoria. You should listen. Come on."

They hurried back down into the tunnels, Diesel leading the way and using his staff as a light. The fairy had flitted off. Victoria wondered if she should have made her stay with them to get an update. *Too late.*

Before long, Diesel led them to some steps carved into the rock. The short stairway ended at a trap door in the ceiling. With a wave of Diesel's hand, it opened enough for him to peek through.

Through the opening, Victoria saw Bertha's store. Heavy footsteps pounded across the hardwood, and the ogre's feet appeared in the gap. The door swung violently open, and Bertha stood ready with a bow and arrow aimed at them.

"It's nice to see you too," Victoria said, crossing her arms.

Bertha relaxed the weapon, and a smile broke across her face. "You three are a sight for sore eyes. Come in."

Before they climbed out, Bertha closed every curtain. The house became dark, lit only by a few lamps on the table or suspended from the ceiling. She nudged the rug back over the trap door to hide it.

"What's going on, Bertha?" Audrey asked as she dusted off her hands.

Bertha opened her mouth to speak, but she paused the

moment her eyes met Audrey's. It was as though the ogre *couldn't* speak. As though the words had been stolen from her mouth. Eventually, Bertha stuttered, "D-dear, you look b-beautiful."

Victoria studied Audrey, and she had to agree. Audrey's dark hair still had the silky sheen of the Atlanteans, and her skin had a healthy silver glow. She had retained the changes even after leaving Atlantis. To her credit, Audrey shuffled a bit awkwardly. "Thank you?"

Bertha nodded, walking about in her kitchen in a daze and occasionally shooting a glance at Audrey as the ogre set out food.

Audrey leaned toward Victoria. "Is that a compliment? Considering how often she called us ugly when we first got here, I'm not sure."

Victoria chuckled.

Bertha took the seat at the head of the table. "You are in grave danger, Victoria. As are you, Audrey, but Victoria is Luak's prime target."

Victoria's smile faded. "He's back?"

Bertha nodded. "He paid me a visit."

Victoria balled her hands into fists to contain her anger. "Did he hurt you?"

The ogre tilted her head and quirked an eyebrow. The expression said, "What the fuck do you think?"

"I'll kill that bastard," Victoria declared.

"No, what you need to do now is stay out of sight," Bertha said.

Diesel leaned against the wall, arms crossed. "How bad is it?"

Bertha chewed her lip, seemingly lost in thought. "Bad.

The king hasn't left his castle. He's made a few appearances to assure us that everything's fine, but he stays on his balcony. He is scared, and so are we. We don't think Luak has made it into the castle yet, but it's inevitable. That's the seat of power in Fairhaven, and Luak wants that power. All of us need to hide."

"Well, we're not leaving the city," Victoria said in a determined voice.

"We absolutely should," Bertha said.

Victoria shook her head. "I'm not going to abandon Fairhaven. We can hide here. Bertha, I need you to find us another home to buy with cash, so no one knows who owns it. We have to stay out of sight, so find something near the tunnels or with trapdoor access like yours. I want to be able to quickly and easily move in and out if need be."

Bertha nodded. "I will make that happen."

The ogre stood and disappeared into one of her back rooms, and Victoria took a chance and headed into the sales area out front. Carefully, she peered through the curtain to find the Main Street empty except for a few hulking silhouettes in the distance. She couldn't make out what race they were, but she did notice the giant axes they carried.

"Looks pretty bad," Audrey said over her shoulder.

Victoria flinched, caught off-guard by Audrey's stealth, but she nodded. "Sure does."

"Are you sure staying is the right idea?"

"Sure am. After all, I have an Atlantean host for a side-kick. How could I lose?" She winked.

Audrey laughed and shoved her in the shoulder, but Victoria couldn't bring herself to smile. Luak had invaded her city, and it seemed as though he was slowly gaining control of it. But this was her home now, and she would be damned if she'd allow Luak to steal *two* homes from her.

Victoria would stay. She would fight. And she would kill that bastard.

The End of Book Two.

Victoria & Audrey are back in Ember, Fairhaven Chronicles book 3, available now at Amazon and through Kindle Unlimited.

A lot has happened in the Oriceran Universe since the last author notes for the Fairhaven Chronicles. The sweetest one was having two bestsellers on Amazon at the same time – and Glow, Book One – was one of them.

That's all thanks to YOU GUYS – the FANS! You guys are rockin' and rollin' with all the new books, still asking for more!

There are now five series launched with 15 books so far and two more new series to come at the start of the year. We've gone from a new Universe to an established playground of great stories with Wizards, Elves and Nichts in just over 90 days.

A BIG THANK YOU to all of you readers for going on this ride with us and letting us know how much you have loved GLOW.

Today, as I write this, is momentous for me in other ways as well. Tomorrow the offspring turns 30! A big deal for both of us.

I still remember the days before he was born. I watched

his Dad finish a marathon and I set up his entire nursery, putting away the tiny clothes. I thought I was finishing early... Louie wasn't due for another six weeks.

He had different plans and was born a preemie weighing in at 8 pounds 12 ounces with bright red curly hair. People were coming over to the NICU window to look at the giant baby in an incubator.

Now, he's well over six feet and blonde curly hair and one of the most generous people I know. Never thought this career of mine was crazy even though there were plenty of years where the budget was so tight it squeaked.

So that's two things to celebrate that have grown up to be something great – one super fast and the other right on time!

CONNECT WITH THE AUTHORS

Martha Carr Social

Website:
http://www.marthacarr.com

Facebook:
https://www.facebook.com/groups/MarthaCarrFans/

https://www.facebook.com/terranavisuniverse/

Michael Anderle Social

Michael Anderle Social
Website:
http://www.lmbpn.com

Email List:
http://lmbpn.com/email/

Facebook
https://www.facebook.com/TheKurtherianGambitBooks/